THE SPIRIT
OF THE RANGE

**Center Point
Large Print**

**This Large Print Book carries the
Seal of Approval of N.A.V.H.**

THE SPIRIT OF THE RANGE

B. M. BOWER

CENTER POINT PUBLISHING
THORNDIKE, MAINE

This Center Point Large Print edition
is published in the year 2005 by arrangement with
Golden West Literary Agency.

Copyright © 1940 by B. M. Bower.
Copyright © renewed 1968 by Dele Newman Doke.

The text of this Large Print edition is unabridged. In other
aspects, this book may vary from the original edition. Printed in
Thailand. Set in 16-point Times New Roman type.

ISBN 1-58547-570-X

Library of Congress Cataloging-in-Publication Data

Bower, B. M., 1874-1940.
    The spirit of the range / B. M. Bower.--Center Point large print ed.
    p. cm.
    ISBN 1-58547-570-X (lib. bdg. : alk. paper)
    1. Large type books. I. Title.

PS3503.O8193S68 2005
813'.52--dc22

                                                            2004020928

CHAPTER ONE

IT WAS four o'clock in the afternoon. Back in the days when the Flying U ran their cattle on the open range between the Missouri and Milk Rivers and a good fifty miles east and west of the Bear Paw Mountains, four o'clock meant suppertime.

Gathering cattle in that large a territory took some riding in the course of a day, and when breakfast is eaten before dawn, four-o'clock supper becomes mighty important. When fifteen hungry cowboys ride into camp to find there is no supper—that is tragedy.

It was easy in such a crisis to tell who were the extra men hired for the season. They stood around in various attitudes of dejection, blank helplessness written all over them. Other long-legged fellows with spurs ajingle hurried in and out of the cook-tent, shouting questions and commands which no one heeded. They were the old hands, frequently referred to as Jim Whitmore's Happy Family.

Not that they were always happy—certainly not on this day—but because through thick and thin they stuck together, and loyalty to the Flying U was so much a part of them they were not conscious of any particular loyalty. As a matter of course they rose to this emergency.

Happy Jack was fanning with his hat a sickly blaze in the sheet-iron stove. His face was red and gloomy at the prospect of having to satisfy so many outdoor appetites on short notice. He was not much of a cook and he hated the job anyway. Now and then he stopped fanning to peer behind the stove where old Patsy, the cook, writhed and groaned upon a hastily unrolled bed.

"What the devil's the matter with that hot water?" Cal Emmett cried urgently. "Ain't that teakettle boiled yet?"

"Aw, fire ain't got a good start yet," Happy Jack looked up to say. "And there ain't no water. Teakettle was bone dry. I sent somebody to the crick for a bucket of water, but looks like he's waitin' to dig a well."

"Well, gee whiz! If it was you tied up in a knot with cramps, you wouldn't be so darned serene about it."

"Aw, gwan! I ain't serene! Not when I gotta cook chuck for this here layout. Patsy ain't got enough stuff cooked up to feed a jackrabbit. Somebody's gotta mosey in here and peel some spuds. I can't do it all."

"That's your funeral," Cal retorted unfeelingly. "Boil 'em with the jackets on, why don't you?"

Chip stuck his head under the lifted tent flap. "Say, I can't find that bottle of Three H," he complained. "What was done with it, Cal?"

"Ask Slim, why don't you? He's the one had it last." Cal turned again to Patsy. "Stay with it, old-timer. We'll get a hot drink down yuh in a minute."

"Fine time to git a bellyache!" Happy Jack grumbled, taking his somber gaze from the licking tongues of flame that showed in the stove front.

Old Patsy struggled for speech. "Py gosh—it's a poison!" He made heartrending sounds, clasping his hands tightly over his paunch. "Can corn," he managed to gasp.

Cal Emmett looked at him wide-eyed, muttered something about seeing what had become of that bucket of water, and got up and left the tent with the ominous news. "The old boy's up against it good and plenty," he announced gravely to those outside. "Ptomaine poisoning. Lays it to the corn."

"He had it comin'," Jack Bates declared unfeelingly. "He's shoved that darned canned corn under our noses every meal since roundup started, and what was left over he packed around in a lard bucket and warmed it up next meal. We'd all of been poisoned if we'd touched the darned stuff."

"Oh, shut up!" Cal snarled at him. "He's liable to cash in, and that won't be so funny." His round, baby-blue eyes glared at the little group. "Tin-can poison sure is fierce."

The faces of the Happy Family lengthened, and they cast uneasy glances at one another. For men of the range, forced to eat largely from tin cans, and seldom being within riding distance of a doctor, dread ptomaine poisoning more than the bite of a rattlesnake. A rattler warns you of his presence; and you never knew what dire suffering might follow a can opener. But since one must eat, and canned vegetables are better than no vegetables at all, the Happy Family ate and took their chance—except that they did not eat canned corn, and they had often discussed their prejudice profanely with old Patsy.

But it happened that Patsy liked canned corn. Never had he stocked the mess wagon for a long trip without including at least two cases of corn. Never did he serve a supper without a big basin of it simmering on the stove. Sometimes the extra men ate it, which encouraged him to go on opening can after can. What spoiled went to

7

feed the gophers—but apparently he had not been generous enough at this camp, and so was paying the price of his greed.

"Ain't there anything you can give him?" Jack Bates repented sufficiently to inquire. "A good jolt of that Three-H liniment oughta fix him up, all right."

"Well, dig it up, somebody!" Cal snapped. "We've got to do something, or we'll have a dead cook on our hands."

"Mamma! If we even had some whisky!" Weary Davidson lamented. "Slim, you oughta be shot for losing that liniment!"

Slim was too downhearted to resent the tone. "By golly, I can't think what I done with it after I used it on Banjo. Seems like I set it on that rock by the corral—"

"Gee whiz!" snorted Cal. "That rock's forty miles back along the trail."

The muffled groans within the tent rose into a prolonged howl.

"Say, it's a fright!" Cal was sweating with excitement. "Ain't there *anything* that'll cure tin-canitis?"

"We need a doctor," Chip stated, pawing through boxes of supplies in a hopeless search for the Three-H bottle. "There goes the darned butter—pick it up, Cal."

"Maybe I better ride into Dry Lake and get Old Doc," Weary suggested worriedly. "What do you think, Chip?"

"He could send out some stuff, anyway—if he's sober enough. That old boy stood ace-high back in France, they tell me. Head of a hospital, the way I heard it. Got in some jam and migrated over to this country."

Chip listened to a horrific crescendo of sound, and

shook his head. "About one chance in a hundred you'll find him sober enough to do any good," he muttered pessimistically. Chip had lately been promoted to roundup boss, and he took his responsibilities seriously.

Weary made himself a cigarette with swift precision. "Well, it's me for Dry Lake," he said. "I reckon Patsy can hang on till I get back; ptomaine's kinda lingering, from all I've heard. It doesn't do the business right off—it takes several hours. He was all right when Happy hit camp about three o'clock, so he's got four or five hours to go, anyway, don't you think?"

"You can search me," Chip replied succinctly.

"I'll be back by dark," Weary promised as he swung up on the nearest horse, which happened to be Chip's. "I'll ride Glory." He wheeled and raced out to the saddle bunch, a quarter of a mile away.

The Happy Family stood and watched him go, faint hope in their eyes. In a surprisingly short time the saddle horses came trotting into camp and were corralled without waste of time. Weary went in among them with his rope down, cannily squinting here and there and everywhere save at Glory, who stood head up and ears tipped forward, watching him suspiciously. For it was always a duel of wits between Weary and that beautiful bright sorrel with the silver mane and tail which Weary claimed as his own private horse and loved in spite of his unpredictable moods. Glory was smart, and Weary loved brains, whether in man or beast; and getting Glory to do what he wanted him to do was always a special private triumph.

"I betcha he don't git Glory," gloomed Happy Jack

who had come out to watch. "Why don't he pick a horse that's dependable?"

"'Cause he wants a fast one," Cal Emmett retorted.

For once Glory was caught off guard. When the noose hissed out over the backs of the other horses, Glory dodged a second too late and found himself neatly caught. It was unusual but he let it pass. He submitted quietly enough to being saddled, merely nipping Weary's shoulder once, and striking out playfully with a front foot—neither of which assaults Weary took seriously. In fact, he was scarcely aware of them, and his silence impressed the horse as no vituperation could have done.

Without a word of praise or blame, Weary swung into the saddle; and Glory, seeming to understand that this was something very urgent, bolted off up the long, western slope of the creek-bottom and disappeared like a scared antelope. For a couple of miles he kept that pace unbroken, though the way was not smooth and there was no trail to follow.

Straight off to the west, with fifteen miles of hills and coulees between, lay the little shipping town of Dry Lake. And there lived the one man in the country who might save Patsy.

As Chip had observed, Old Doc was something of a mystery and a landmark in the country. The oldest pioneer claimed to have found Doc there before him, dosing the Indians when they gorged themselves too recklessly after a big kill of buffalo or came to grief among the many hazards of the plains. He was a fresh-faced young Frenchman then, they said, and his knowledge of medicine seemed limitless. From the Indians he had learned the use of strange herbs that healed almost with magic speed and certainty; from the bullwhackers and traders he learned to drink vile concoctions called whisky by courtesy and to call it good.

Dry Lake, which grew up around him, could not remember Doc as anything but a white-whiskered, stooped little old man whose mild, wrinkled hands could set a broken bone with incredible gentleness, drunk or sober.

When his bouts of drinking were sufficiently spaced to leave brief periods of sober judgment between, they called him in preference to Great Falls doctors—and not always in a spirit of economy either.

And one reason why men trusted him was that nothing could induce him to prescribe medicine when drunk. It was the firm belief of many that he could "knock the spots off" any other doctor in northern Montana when he was "at himself"; so while they made him the butt of their crude jokes, and held him in amused contempt as the town drunkard, nevertheless they trusted him for his skill.

When Weary galloped up the wide dusty roadway which was the only street Dry Lake possessed—all others being mere rutted trails branching off to suit the convenience of the inhabitants—he was gambling on the slim chance that Old Doc would be sober. His eyes sought impatiently for the familiar figure of the old man. Minutes were precious and he was not in the mood to waste any of them—even pushing from his mind the fact that his stomach was howling for food and that a mere glass of beer would be most welcome.

With sure instinct he pulled up before the porch of Rusty Brown's saloon, where a group of possibly a dozen men were laughing uproariously. It was not until he had dismounted at the hitching pole and pushed up the steps that he saw what had caused the hilarity.

Old Doc stood in the center of the group, trembling with rage. With both hands he held up a greenish-black coat to show the world two sheets of Tanglefoot flypaper plastered on the back.

"Dat vass by meanness," he was declaring, his gentle old voice shrill with anger. "Me, I'm never do de harm wiss no mans. Always I'm mind mine business. I buy me mine clothes. De man w'at do dese treeck, *he* buys me new clothes, you bet you! You tell me what mans—"

"Oh, say, Doc," Weary broke in, laying a hand on the old doctor's shoulder. "You're just the one I'm looking for. Our cook's awful sick out in camp. Dig up something for tin-can poison, will you?"

Bleared eyes squinted up at him as Old Doc shook his shaggy white head. "You see dat? Mine coat, he's ruint. I don't do harm wiss any mans! Dat was mean treeck!"

"Yeah, it sure was, all right. The fellow that did that oughta buy you a new coat, that's a cinch. But, Doc, listen! Tell me what's good for tin-can poison."

"Ah, you fellers t'ink ol' Doc she don' know nawthin'! You t'ink Ol' Doc—"

Weary turned palms outward and swung on the laughing crowd. "Say, which end of a jag is this?" he demanded with exasperation. "Is he just started on one, or just tapering off? I rode fifteen miles to pry some

12

information outa Doc somehow. I can't go back without it. Old Patsy's a goner, sure, if I don't get right back there with some medicine for tin-can poison!"

Everyone knew Patsy, who was almost as much a landmark as was Old Doc. And it certainly was gratifying to see how that bunch crowded up to hear how it had happened. But Patsy needed something more potent than sympathy, and the minutes were passing.

Old Doc stood there and discoursed eloquently upon the subject of his ruined coat and the ingratitude of Dry Lake. Though Weary begged and pleaded with him, he could not win the old man's attention. And in that befuddled brain was locked the knowledge that might save old Patsy's life. It was maddening.

"Look, Doc! I'll *buy* you a new coat! Now, tell me what's good for tin-can poison! You know—*ptomaine!* Patsy's got it, and you're the only man this side of Fort Benton that knows what to do for him!"

"Ol' Doc fine for keeds—fine for save life when de beeg seekness come—fine for sit all night by dying mans—fine to play de mean treeck for grin!"

And that was all the satisfaction Weary could get from him.

CHAPTER TWO

WEARY'S HAND dropped in despair from Old Doc's shoulder. He turned, went down the steps and swung into the saddle. "Rusty, I want to borrow that calico cayuse of yours. Have him saddled up right away, will you? I'll be back in ten minutes."

He jerked his hat down to his eyebrows, wheeled Glory sharply around and galloped off. But the trail he presently took was strange to Glory, who felt impelled to stop and argue—as only Glory knew how to argue—with his master.

Minutes passed tumultuously, with nothing accomplished save some weird hoofprints in the sod. Presently, however, since Weary was a terribly stubborn young man once he made up his mind, Glory permitted himself to be reined into a dim trail that wound down into a grassy swale, up out of that, up over a ridge and down a long slope on the other side to a low-eaved cabin set snugly on the sunny side of a small basin half a mile from town.

By nature and by habit Weary was a most law-abiding person, though in emergencies he could sweep aside technicalities as ruthlessly as any man. He opened the door of the cabin and went in with no compunctions whatever.

The interior was dark and none too clean, and the air was close and smelled strongly of herbs and antiseptics; but after the first gasp he scarcely noticed the indescribable odor. He didn't know exactly what he was looking for, except that he had to find Doc's medicine. The bunches of herbs tied and hanging from the ridgepole he passed by after one glance. He wanted something stronger than that for old Patsy.

An old-fashioned chest set against the wall looked promising, but it was padlocked, and he left that as a last resort while he searched elsewhere for what he wanted. Under the bed he finally discovered a flat black case such as old-fashioned doctors carried. He drew it out and examined it critically. This, too, was locked, but when he shook it gently he heard a faint clinking sound inside, and gave a grunt of satisfaction.

"Bottles," he said aloud. Old Doc's medicine case, without a doubt. And he turned toward the door before he reconsidered and pulled down the nearest bunch of herbs from the ridgepole. These he tucked into his coat pocket and mounted for the homeward ride.

The sun was low and even before he reached the town, riding swiftly, the sky was suffused with the garish purple, red and orange of sunset. Old Doc was still gesticulating wildly, and one sheet of flypaper still clung to the back of his coat. The crowd had thinned somewhat; otherwise the situation remained the same, except that a pinto pony stood meekly at the hitch-pole.

"There's your horse," Rusty called out through the open doorway. "What's the matter with that sorrel? Played out?"

"Not on your life!" Weary retorted. "When you see Glory played out, you see him with all four feet in the air."

"That's nothing," Bert Rogers bantered. "I saw him that way half an hour ago."

Aghast at the passage of time, Weary ignored the joke. "Mamma! Have I been here half an hour?" He swung off and went up to the old man. "Here, Doc, you put on that coat and never mind the label. Wait, I'll peel it off for you. You'll have to go with me to camp, see?"

"Ah, he's no good to you, Weary," Bert Rogers

15

protested. "He's too drunk to tell chloroform from dried apples."

"He won't be, by the time he hits camp," Weary made grim reply. "I went down and dug up his medicine case so he can start right in on Patsy the minute he gets there. The ride in the fresh air will sober him up, all right. Come on, Bert, help me boost him into the saddle."

Rusty Brown came out on the porch, wiping his hands on his almost-white apron. "Say, you ain't goin' to put Doc on Powderface, are yuh?" His eyes held consternation. "I thought you was goin' to ride him yourself. Old Doc couldn't ride that horse even when he's sober. It's plumb wicked to put the old centurion on him the way he is—he wouldn't be able to stay with that horse a mile!"

"That's farther than he would get on Glory," Weary retorted imperturbably. "You don't seem to realize, none of you fellows, that Patsy's due to croak if he don't get help."

"You can skin me for a coyote if you get any help from that old booze-hound, the state he's in," Rusty declared vehemently.

"The way he is now ain't going to be the way he'll land in camp," Weary patiently pointed out as he led the old man down the steps. "Doc's got the cure for Patsy sloshing around in all that whisky in his head. I can't wait for him to sober up here—I'm just going to take him along, jag and all. Come on, Doc. This is a lovely evening for a ride. Make you feel good."

Old Doc made emphatic objections with head, arms, legs and much mixed dialect, but with the help of Bert

16

Rogers, Weary lifted him bodily into the saddle. When the pinto began to snort and sidle, Bert shook his head dubiously.

"He'll tumble off, sure as you're born," he predicted, but Weary grinned a little and untied his rope from his own saddle.

"By the lord Harry! I sure hate to see a man ride into town and pack off the only heirloom we got," Rusty Brown complained from the porch. "Old Doc's been handed down from generation to Genesis, and there ain't hardly a scratch on 'im. You'd better bring him back in good condition, Weary Davidson—now I'm telling yuh!"

Weary was doing an expert job of roping Old Doc to the saddle. He looked up from taking the last half-hitch around the saddlehorn and a cold chill ran up his spine. For here came Joe Meeker who lived up near the schoolhouse which served the ranchers near the Flying U. Joe was driving his best team hitched to his top buggy, and the new schoolma'am was with him.

Joe slowed the horses to a walk, and yelled facetiously to Weary. "What you doin' to Old Doc, Weary? Takin' him home to raise, or what?"

"Don't lay awake worrying," Weary retorted, wanting to choke Joe Meeker—always trying to show off before a girl. Weary was girl-shy, and the bright stare of the schoolma'am was more than he could face.

He turned his back on the two and spoke gruffly to Rusty Brown. "Doc's more valuable to me than he is to you, right now. I'll get him there if I have to carry him in my arms!"

"Dat vass de mean treeck!" Doc reiterated, blinking at the rope. "Mine coat she iss ruint, an' now I don't like for ride some place. Dass mean treeck!"

"It sure is," Weary muttered, slanting a glance over his shoulder to make sure Joe had driven on. It didn't help much to see the new schoolma'am leaning out so that she could continue to stare back at him. She had her nerve—more nerve than manners, he told himself resentfully.

He tied the pinto's bridle-reins into a hard knot at the end, and with the reins in his hand, he mounted Glory. "Say, this cayuse will lead all right, won't he?" he asked Rusty, just to convince himself the girl couldn't rattle him.

"I dunno. He never did, far's I ever heard." Rusty grinned maliciously. "I wouldn't be none surprised if you found out before yuh got there."

Old Doc made a last, futile effort to free himself, then settled down in the saddle and sulked, eying his world sullenly from under his shaggy white brows. They started off tamely enough, considering.

The pinto pulled back on the reins and trotted with stiff, reluctant legs, but he went; and Weary drew a relieved breath. He had lost a little time, one way and another, here in town; but the boys would do all they could until he got there with help. He began to feel more hopeful for Patsy.

Although it was early fall, the weather had been warm, with occasional rains, and the twilight was soft and warm as a July evening when they started up the four-mile lane through the meadowland which lay between town and the first line of hills.

Over by the creek, frogs made tuneful chorus. Nighthawks glided silently through the still air, swooping downward with a queer, whooing rush, like wind blowing briefly through a cavern. Once well into the lane, the faint, insistent humming of millions of hardy mosquitoes made the air vibrant with sound.

Only too well Weary knew that ominous humming, and he touched Glory with the spurs and came near having his arm jerked from its socket before he could pull him up again. He swung around in the saddle and looked back.

"Kick that cayuse into a lope, won't you, Doc?" he called. "We're going to be just naturally chewed up if we don't fan a breeze up along here."

"Dass vass de meanest treeck!" Old Doc shouted querulously.

Weary opened his mouth, came near swallowing several mosquitoes and closed it hastily. He waited until the pinto came up alongside, then struck him sharply with his quirt. The pinto shied away, causing Doc to lurch drunkenly in the saddle.

"Come along, then!" Weary gritted under his breath, and gave another yank on the reins.

Whereupon the pinto snorted and ran backward a few paces, Weary clinging to the reins. Then the mosquitoes swooped down in a cloud upon them, and Glory struck out, fighting and kicking viciously. With one hand Weary sought to control the maddened brute, and with the other he tried to yank the pinto along; and between the two he felt as if he were being pulled apart.

19

Then suddenly the terrific strain on his arm gave way. He found himself with part of the pinto's bridle-reins in his hand, and the memory of Old Doc bouncing grotesquely in the saddle as the pinto disappeared into the darkness ahead.

There was nothing he could do about it at the moment, since Glory was wholeheartedly engaged in trying to buck off mosquitoes faster than they could land, and to confuse them further by bucking in a circle. Weary rode out the storm, thanking the good Lord that Old Doc and the pinto were headed in the right direction up the lane. Every mile they covered added to Patsy's chance of pulling through, and when he could, Weary gave chase exultantly.

Even the mosquitoes were hopelessly out-distanced as they galloped steadily through the lane towards the hills. Doc couldn't get away, and he couldn't fall off, roped as he was, so it really was a big relief when the pinto made up his mind to travel.

Presently another small discomfort threatened to become a sizable problem. It was the black medicine case tied to the fork of the saddle. At first he hadn't noticed it knocking against his leg as he rode, but like the well-known drop of water, the sharp corner of that case began to grow into torture. He thought of tying it flat behind the cantle, but he had nothing with which to pad it, and he was pretty certain that Glory would like those sharp corners even less than he did. He left the case where it was.

As he left the lane behind him, he sighted the pinto and Doc just disappearing up a coulee which led nowhere—

much less to camp. Weary swung in after them. Two miles farther along, where the coulee ended abruptly in rock ledges and steep shale slopes which a coyote couldn't have climbed, he was much surprised to find no pinto and no Doc; though where they could have gotten to, he could not imagine.

From side to side he searched that coulee fruitlessly. The thought of old Patsy's suffering haunted him. Later, he thought of poor Old Doc, lashed to the pinto's saddle; and his conscience berated him unmercifully for the thing he had done and the risk he had taken with one man's life on the off-chance of saving another.

Night had fallen and a cool breeze had sprung up, and there was poor little Old Doc, tied to a horse and lost in these hills. Anything could happen to the old man; and whatever did happen, he'd be the one to blame for it. It didn't make pleasant thinking.

CHAPTER THREE

DOWN NEAR the mouth of the coulee a scarcely perceptible cattle trail angled up the steep slope toward the stars. It didn't seem likely that the pinto had chosen that laborious climb rather than follow the level coulee bottom to its end, but Weary reflected that you never know just what a strange horse will do when left to his own devices; and he took that trail.

Up on top of the rolling benchland the prairie stretched mysteriously away under the sky, with no sound to mar the broody silence of the night nor any movement save that made by Glory and himself. All that day the hills had been buffeted by a sweeping west wind, but, with the setting of the sun, that had softened to a breeze, and by dark it had died to a calm silence.

An Indian trick occurred to Weary. He got off his horse and knelt with one ear pressed against the ground. A galloping horse would have been heard for a long way, but there was nothing to show that any other animal walked within a mile of him.

He mounted again, shifting the medicine case to ease his bruised leg; and he wished that he could have carried Old Doc's brain, with all the knowledge it held, to camp with him along with the medicine case. That would have simplified matters, if he could have looked into the brain and found just what was needed for ptomaine, got the stuff out of the case and dosed old Patsy himself.

It was an intriguing thought and he played with it for a while as he rode slowly up along the coulee's rim, listening vainly for strange hoofbeats.

He regretted now that he had not learned from Rusty Brown more about the pinto's habits and natural preferences. Undoubtedly, the horse had come from some ranch originally, and if left to himself would return there.

Or he might go back to Dry Lake—that is, unless he happened to be a horse with no natural instincts for home nor any imagination; in which case he might wander around aimlessly all night, or even fall over a cut-bank. Old Doc wouldn't know enough to guide him in any given direction, or if he did sober up enough for that, he couldn't do much without bridle-reins.

Weary was notoriously sweet-tempered, and men marveled at his patience. He was even called the peacemaker of the Flying U outfit, and the general belief was that nothing could rile him to the point of being anything less than just. But after he had ridden an uneven course over that rough foothill country, with his worry over old Patsy, his empty stomach and his gouged leg to keep him unwelcome company, his good temper suddenly exploded into muttered denunciation of his horse.

"You darn taffy-colored cayuse," he cried with a bitterness that made Glory jump and dance off sidewise, "you started all this, now why don't you finish it? Got so darned touchy back there in the lane you couldn't stand for a few mosquito bites! Had to put on a show over it. Had to go and bust the pinto's bridle and scare him plumb out of the country!

"If anything happens to Old Doc, *you're* the one responsible for it, not me. I was doing all right till you went and got delicate all of a sudden over a few mosquitoes—and darn your measly hide, you came down that lane a hundred times with the mosquitoes so thick you had to break trail like plowing through a snowdrift! It ain't as if you'd never been bit before!

"You pride yourself on your smartness; why don't you get smart enough to find that pinto? This is as much your funeral as it is mine—and don't you forget it! You lost him, now find him. Get a move on, you knock-kneed, buzzard-headed old pelter! Think I'm going to let you amble around out here all night, like an old cow going to pasture? You get busy and find that horse you lost, or I'll beat the hide off you!"

This was manifestly unjust and it was also very unlike Weary. He leaned and shifted the medicine case again,

23

and rubbed his bruised leg. "Mamma!" he muttered in deep disgust. "This is certainly a sarcastic night! Dope enough here to cure all the sickness in the country, if a fellow only knew how to use it—and all it can do is gouge a hole in my leg you could throw a calf through! And the brain that knows how to use it is pickled in rot-gut whisky—and me wanderin' around out here like a locoed sheepherder!"

He sat there staring gloomily into the vague starlight, mentally debating whether to go back to Dry Lake in the hope of finding the pinto there. But if the horse had gone back to town, Old Doc would be taken off by someone. And he'd be so mad he wouldn't even tell Weary what medicine to use. No, going back to town would be worse than useless. All he could do was ride around and trust to luck; which is exactly what he did, though the luck he trusted in most was not good luck, but bad.

The night was far gone and the slant of the Great Dipper told him that dawn was near when he heard a horse whinny wistfully, away off in the distance. Instantly he was wide-awake and sitting straight in the saddle, listening. The sound came again, and he reined Glory halfway around and raced him recklessly in that direction.

As he neared the vague bulk of a horse and rider out-lined against the skyline, Weary's heart came up in his throat and almost choked him; and it was not until that moment that he fully realized how worried he had been. The pinto nickered again, and the squat figure in the saddle moved and spoke angrily:

"If it iss you, Weary Davitson, what for you do dese

t'ings? Dese horse, she lak for keel me also. She buck an' she keek an' run—*mon Dieu,* I don' lak for dese kind of joking!"

"Oh, hello, Doc!" Weary's voice was hollow with embarrassment which he tried to cover by being very cheerful. "How you coming? Sure sorry the pinto broke away from me back there in the lane—remember? I've been looking for you all this time."

"I look for you also, for feex you planty. W'at for you tie dese rope by me? I t'ink also you like for keel me, *n'est-ce pas?*"

Weary had dismounted and was walking up to the pinto very quietly, making soothing talk in a murmuring voice. Not until his hand had come up to the pinto's bridle did he attempt to answer Old Doc. "The rope? Well, you wasn't very steady on your pins last night, you remember—I just wanted to make sure you wouldn't fall off, is all. Didn't know what the pinto might take a notion to do."

"You t'ink I no ride de horse, perhaps?" Old Doc snorted. "I'm riding de must*ang* for hunting buffaloes when you was not born!"

"Oh sure, sure! I know you can ride, Doc. Sure I do." Weary was busy with the pinto's bridle-reins. "I guess I was a little excited last night. Didn't want to stop and argue, on account of old Patsy."

"I'm not mak' argument for Patsy," Old Doc retorted stiffly. "I'm mak' argument for de coat. She's ruint!"

"Yeah, I know. But Doc, you've got a chance to save a life—old Patsy's life—if we ain't too late. You remember where we're headed for, don't you?"

25

"I t'ink for de devil!" Old Doc retorted peevishly.

Weary continued to make his voice very cheerful and reassuring. "No, Doc, we're going to Flying U roundup camp. You're going to save old Patsy's life, if he ain't dead already. You like old Patsy—I've seen you crying on each other's shoulders more than once, and swapping yarns about the Old Country." Weary's persuasiveness was as studied as that employed for a sulky child. "You remember, Doc, I told you last night Patsy got poisoned on canned corn. We'd have been there and had him all cured by now, if this darned pinto hadn't bucked loose."

He had finished toggling the broken reins so that they would hold. "Come on, Doc, we'll have to hit the breeze."

"I not like dese rope. She's not comfort'. I have to ride de mustang—"

Weary was most apologetic. "Excuse me, Doc, I plumb forgot about the rope." And he proceeded to free Doc, unwinding the lashings swiftly. "But you know, Doc, when we started out from town, you wasn't in any condition to ride a rocking chair, even. I just naturally had to tie you on." He peered up anxiously into the old man's face. "You think we'll get there in time? Patsy was taken sick about four o'clock. I don't know when he ate the corn."

Old Doc shook himself like a rumpled bird and gathered up the mended bridle-reins. "I'm not wave de hand and say de mageec word," he snapped. "I mus' have de medezeen or nozing is accomplish'. From four o'clock till now iss long time for ptomaine poison."

"I know," Weary returned dejectedly. "But I've got the

medicine, Doc. I broke into your shack and got the whole works. I knew you'd need medicine to work with, so I took a liberty, I guess. You wouldn't talk about anything but your coat, and I had to think of old Patsy."

"Mon Dieu!" was Old Doc's astonished comment; and after that no more was said, for they were riding fast.

The first rays of sunlight were tinting the hilltops a soft orange and the birds were singing from swaying weeds when they rode down the last slope into the valley where the Flying U camped. The nighthawk had driven the horses into the rope corral and men were inside watching, with spread loops, for a chance to throw.

Happy Jack, with the cook's floursack apron tied tightly around his lank middle, stood disconsolately in the opening of the mess tent, and had no word of greeting for them as they approached. In his silence—in his very presence there—Weary read the worst.

"Looks like we're too late," he told Doc under his breath, and glanced sidelong at the stooped old man whose drunkenness had cost the Flying U so dear. While Happy Jack eyed him woodenly, Weary swung down from the saddle and let Glory's reins drop to the ground. "Well?" he asked when the silence became unbearable.

"When I git sick," Happy Jack said heavily, "I'll send *you* for help—I don't think!"

"When—how long ago did it happen?" The tightness in Weary's throat filled him with a dull surprise. He never had realized before that there was any affection in his heart for old Patsy, and it gave him a queer sensation not to be able to ask straight out when Patsy had died.

Happy Jack continued to stare at him reproachfully.

27

"Was it poker or billiards?" His voice was heavy with sarcasm.

"Neither one. We've been all night getting here."

"Aw, gwan! I betcha you got into a game and forgot to jar loose, till most morning. It sure ain't no thanks to you 't old Patsy ain't croaked long ago!"

Weary stared blankly for a moment before the full import of that statement penetrated his consciousness. With a pronounced limp in his leg from the gouging of the medicine case, he pulled a crumpled, faintly aromatic bundle from his coat pocket and walked over to where Doc stood leaning shakily against the pinto.

"Looks like we're in time, after all," he said. "Here's some stuff I pulled down from the ceiling; thought you might need it, Doc. I know you learned lots of tricks about herbs from the Indians."

Old Doc took the bundle, glanced at it contemptuously and dropped it on the ground. "W'at you t'ink? You t'ink mebbe I cure poison wit' *catneep?* Dass for de leetle small baby, sometime." He smiled sourly beneath his beard.

"How in thunder should I know what the blamed stuff was?" Weary cast a furtive glance at Happy Jack, hoping he had not overheard. He limped back to Glory, untied the black medicine case and brought it and put it at the feet of Old Doc. "Well, here's the joker, anyhow," he said grimly. "It like to wore a hole clear through my leg, but I was careful not to jounce it much and I don't believe any of the bottles got busted."

"De joker?" Old Doc gave him a sharp glance and sat down abruptly on an upturned box. He squinted down at

28

the black case, then lifted his shaggy head and looked at Weary. Something very like a twinkle appeared in his bleared eyes.

"Me, I'm t'ink dese iss de beeg joke. I'm t'ink Patsy she is not cure from ptomaine from *dat* med'zeen. Iss mos' unfortunate." He leaned and touched a tiny spring in the bag which Weary had not discovered. (Indeed, he had not tried very hard to discover it.) Doc laid the case open on the ground.

"You see?" Old Doc spread both hands in a gesture of helplessness, and looked plaintively into Weary's face. "She not cure for Patsy. She not good instrument for operate on nawthings but tin can!"

Weary stared dazedly down upon the case, in his stupefaction permitting Happy Jack to shoulder him aside as he came up. His mind simply refused to credit the reality of the thing he gazed upon.

"*Can openers!*" shouted Happy Jack. "Hey, Chip! What you know about this? Weary's went and brung a suitcase full of *can openers* to doctor Patsy's bellyache!"

Men came running. "By golly, it'd serve the old devil right if Doc went to work on 'im with 'em!" Slim bellowed as he waddled up.

Old Doc stood up and began explaining in his best English. "She iss de new kind. I'm t'ink mebbe I sell. I'm put her in de case—mine med'zeen, she iss in de beeg chest."

Weary's shoulders sagged and his hands dropped dejectedly at his sides. "Well, I could make another trip in after what you need, if you think it's any use," he offered dispiritedly. "Better go and look him over while

I swallow a cup of coffee and saddle a fresh horse. I'll get that medicine out here if it's the last thing I do on earth!"

"Aw, gwan!" Happy Jack snorted. "That old Dutchman don't need no medicine. Right after you left last night, a sheepman rode into camp and he had a quart bottle on his hip. Chip begged it off'n him and give Patsy a good stiff jolt. That eased him up, but he hollered for more—"

"Yeah. And by golly, he hollered off 'n' on as long as there was a drop left. You got anything for snakes, by golly—"

Happy Jack took up the tale. "Yeah. An' *I* had to cook supper an' breakfast too! Looks like I'll have t' cook dinner if somebody don't do something about soberin' Patsy up. Poison—hell!"

Weary left them laughing over the can openers and the catnip, and went to the mess tent; lifted the flap and looked in upon Patsy lying on the flat of his back, snoring in complete, hoggish comfort and a disreputable peace.

For a long minute Weary stood there surveying the scene. But what he saw—and he couldn't account for it at the time—was the curious, shocked face of the new schoolma'am staring back at him there at the hitch-rail while he roped Old Doc to the saddle of that walleyed pinto. "Mamma!" he whispered in deep embarrassment and turned away to the stove to pour himself a cup of coffee.

CHAPTER FOUR

THE STORY got around, as such stories will. Weary took his medicine with a grin, though it did irk him considerably to know that that darned schoolma'am must have heard it with all the variations. What Joe Meeker would add to the can openers for good measure, Weary preferred not to contemplate.

He preferred not to think of the schoolma'am at all, for that matter, for he was notoriously girl-shy. But her face kept coming into his thoughts at the most unexpected times, and when it did she was always looking back at him from Joe Meeker's top buggy. Her mouth was always puckered up at the scene of a tall young cow-puncher winding rope around a very drunken old man with a bushy white beard, so he couldn't fall off the horse; and her eyes, as Weary remembered them, were always wide open with surprise and disapproval. Brown eyes, he thought they were; dark brown and very bright and sparkling, taking in everything within range, especially things she was not supposed to see.

Weary didn't like it. He was glad they were on roundup and wouldn't be riding anywhere near Joe Meeker's place where she boarded, or the Meeker schoolhouse where she taught assorted sizes of young Beckmans and Pilgreens and Meekers, with a few odd ones he didn't know so well. He hoped he wouldn't have to meet her after roundup was over. He didn't see how he was ever going to face her.

But the joke finally wore itself out, as jokes always do,

give them time enough. The Happy Family had said everything they could think of concerning can openers as a cure for colic, and Weary saw peace ahead. He could retire into the background of men's minds and they wouldn't have to strain themselves any longer to be funny whenever they saw him. The relief was tremendous. Weary came out of his shell and the Happy Family resumed their normal, good-humored bickering.

Then something happened which, though it seemed only a casual incident at the time, proved later to have been an event of prime importance to the Flying U. It was nothing less than an addition to their number, and since his coming had a direct and lasting influence on Weary Davidson, the incident deserves its full share of notice.

It happened that the Flying U roundup moved in close to Dry Lake with a beef herd which was to be shipped to Chicago the next day. But prices of beef were so good that shipping was heavy that fall, and the Montana Central was confronted with a temporary famine in stock cars. The train of empties ordered for that certain date by the Flying U had not arrived, and Chip Bennett, still new at the job of being foreman, felt that he had more trouble than he needed right then.

For one thing, he was short-handed, and he needed all of his men to watch those rollicky beef steers until they could be loaded and sent on their way. But two of his crew went on a spree in town; and though they were not top hands, they were needed to help hold the herd. When they were still absent on the second day and there was no word of any cars coming to take the beef steers, Chip saddled a horse and rode into town to fire the shirkers and hire other men in their places.

He had intended to do it quietly and with dignity, as befitted his nature and the outfit he worked for. But two nights and a day of roistering had given those two cowpunchers a false sense of their importance to the outfit. Having spent their money they did not want to be fired—but neither did they want to report back to camp for work. Night-guarding did not appeal to them when they could see the lights of Dry Lake twinkling in the distance.

Nevertheless Chip made his purpose sufficiently plain, and stalked off to consider where he could find two other men to take their places. And it was then that a young fellow with curly golden hair, innocent blue eyes and with dimples in his cheeks when he smiled followed him outside.

"If you're looking for men," he began in a pleasant voice which had melody in its tones, "I'm open for an engagement."

Chip turned and looked down upon him with tolerant amusement. A pink-and-white silk shirt, gray trousers, russet leather belt, panama hat and absurdly small tan shoes marked him as a young dandy from some town much larger than Dry Lake.

"Sorry, but I'm not getting up a garden party," he said shortly, and started on.

"Well, I ain't looking for a job driving cows to pasture, either," the young man boldly retorted. "You shouldn't judge a fellow by his clothes, old-timer."

"I don't—*a man*," Chip said with a slight impatience.

33

"Run along and play, why don't you? I'm not running a kindergarten. Every man I hire has got a man's work to do. I'm afraid you'll have to grow some before you start playing cowboy."

"Is that so! Did you ever hear of old Eagle Creek Smith, of the Cross L, or Rowdy Vaughn, or a fellow up on Milk River they call Pink?"

Chip turned and looked at him more closely then. "Well, I've heard of Eagle Creek Smith and Pink—a bronc fighter, and a devil on wheels. Why—you know them?"

The little fellow lifted his panama hat, ran his fingers through his curls and smiled demurely. "Well, I worked for Eagle Creek Smith—and *I* happen to be Pink."

Chip showed by the look in his eyes that he didn't believe it. He surveyed the slender figure from the accurately dented hat crown to the number-five shoes. "Well, you sure don't look it," he said bluntly. "If you're Milk River Pink, why that elaborate disguise of respectability?"

An empty beer keg stood there in the shade of the saloon. The little fellow sat down on it and rolled a cigarette.

"Well, you see," he began in his soft voice, "when the Cross L moved their stock across the Line, Rowdy Vaughn had charge of the outfit. And we were pretty good friends—so of course I went along.

"Hadn't been over there a month until I had occasion to thump the daylights outa one of them grangers up there, and I put him all to the bad. So a bunch of them gaudy buck policemen rose up and fogged me back

34

across the Line. A man sure has got to turn the other cheek up in Canada, or languish in *ga-ol*." Pink brought out the last word as if it did not taste good.

"Yes, they're pretty law-abiding up there, all right."

"Well, I hit for upper Milk River, but it was so cussed lonesome, with all the old bunch gone, I sold my outfit and quit punching cows—forever, according to me."

He looked like a disgruntled cherub who was just learning to smoke, and Chip had to stifle a laugh. "The puncher doesn't live that hasn't sold his saddle and bed sometime or other, and reformed," he commented dryly.

"Well, I had a fair-sized stake saved up, so I took the home trail back to Minnesota and chewed on the fatted calf all last winter and this summer. It wasn't bad, at first; but it did get blamed monotonous. I dubbed around back there as long as I could stand it, and then I drifted. I kinda got hungry for the feel of a real horse between my legs again.

"Mister, the fences are so thick back there you couldn't get out and fan the breeze if you wanted to. Keeps you busy opening and shutting gates. And every decent bed-ground, where you could bed down a herd and sing 'em to sleep, has got a house and barn stuck on it. For the Lord's sake, stake me to a string of horses! I don't give a damn how rough they are—and show me a herd of cattle!"

Chip sat down on a neighboring keg and eyed the dapper young man curiously. "You're on!" he said laconically. "We've got a heap of work ahead, and only five men in the outfit I can really bank on in a pinch. It's the Flying U; and those five have worked for the outfit for years."

"The Flying U, hunh?" Pink's face brightened and the dimples stood deep in his cheeks. "Say, I've heard of that Flying U Happy Family, all over the country. You're one of them, ain't you?"

Chip grinned, but his eyes were just a shade wistful. "Well, I was," he admitted. "When you get right down to cases, I guess I am, yet. But I went up a notch last spring. Got married and settled down. I'm one of the firm, now, so I had to reform and cut out the foolishness. They're a pretty salty bunch but you'll get along all right—seeing you're not the pilgrim you look to be. If you were, I'd say Lord help you! Got an outfit?"

"Sure. Went to work and bought me a brand-new one up in the Falls. It's over at the hotel now, with a haughty buckskin-colored suitcase that fairly screams with style and newness." Pink pulled his silver belt buckle straight and patted his pink-and-blue tie approvingly. "I went whole hog last fall when I quit, and got rid of everything that would remind me of my guilty past. But it don't matter—I'll darn soon wear the squeaks out of this outfit."

Chip nodded, an odd light in his eyes. "Well, if you're ready, I'll get the horses these two hobos I just fired rode into town, and we'll drift. By the way, how shall I write your name down in the book?"

Pink stooped and with his handkerchief carefully wiped the last of the Dry Lake dust from his shiny tan shoes. "You won't crawfish on me if I tell you?" he inquired, standing up and adjusting his belt again.

"Of course not." Chip looked surprised. "If you're Milk River Pink, that's good enough for me. But I thought you might have a more formal name to use on the payroll."

"Well, it ain't my fault, but so help me Josephine, my lawful, legal name is Percival Cadwallader Perkins."

"Wha-at?"

"Percival Cad-wall-ader Perkins. Shall I get you a drink of water or something to take it with?"

Chip had his book out and, with his pencil poised in the air, he grinned sympathetically. "That's sure a humdinger of a name," he observed. "How do you spell that second one?"

Pink told him, spelling the word slowly, syllable by syllable. "Josephine! Ain't it fierce?" he exclaimed when the name was duly written down in the book. "My mother sure was an obliging lady. I'm the only boy she ever had, and there was two grandfathers on hand arguing that I oughta be named after them. Mother done her darnedest—they sure make a hot combination! You know what Cadwallader means in the dictionary?"

"Lord, no!" said Chip, putting away his book.

"Battle arranger," Pink told him sadly. "Wouldn't that jar you? But it's the truth, too. Cadwallader sure has arranged a lot of battles for me. When I went to school it caused me to lick about six kids a day—and get licked by about a dozen. So, seeing the name belonged to me and I had to live with it, I wasn't more than about fifteen when I throwed in with an ex-pugilist and learned the trade thorough."

"I see," Chip made tactful comment, his eyes resting thoughtfully on Pink. "That accounts for a lot."

"Yeah. And this summer I fell in with a jujitsu shark—a college-fed Jap that sure taught me things a white man never dreamed about. I sat at his feet all summer learning wisdom, and I ain't afraid now to wear Percival Cadwallader on my hatband!"

"Still, I wouldn't," Chip dryly advised him. "Hike over and get the haughty new warbag and we'll hit the trail. I've got to be in camp by dinnertime."

A mile out of Dry Lake, Pink looked down at his festive garments and smiled. "I expect I'll be pickings for your Happy Family when they see me in these glad rags," he observed shyly.

Chip turned and regarded him meditatively for a moment. "I was just wondering," he said slowly, "if the Happy Family won't be pickings for *you?*" He bit his lip and looked away. "Just make yourself at home, Pink—I'll leave you to get acquainted your own way."

"Well, thanks a lot. I guess I'll make out—I always have." Pink's dimples showed briefly, and his indigo eyes were almost too childlike in their innocence. He dropped back a little and rode the rest of the way in silence.

CHAPTER FIVE

THE FLYING U boys were hunkered down on bootheels, or sitting on boxes or bedrolls with their plates in their laps and straight-sided tin cups of coffee handy, eating their dinner all peaceful and serene, when Chip and Pink rode up. Their horses had broken from a lope into a trot as they approached the camp; and Pink, a rod or two behind Chip, was bouncing like a bag of potatoes in the saddle and staring around him curiously.

Mastication temporarily ceased while everyone turned unbelieving eyes upon the dapper little stranger. The two dismounted near the bed-tent (Pink with self-conscious awkwardness) and Chip led the way over to where the boys were sitting. The Happy Family received them, not with the nudges and winks one might expect, but with decorous silence and their gaze tactfully restrained from open staring.

Chip got himself a plate, knife, fork and spoon and started for the stove just inside the cook-tent, out of the wind.

"Help yourself to the cutlery and then come over here and fill up your plate," he invited Pink over his shoulder. "We don't stand on ceremony here. This may look kinda crude and unorganized, but you'll get used to eating with your plate in your lap like a church sociable."

"Yes sir, I know I will. I catch onto things very quickly."

The Happy Family looked guardedly at one another. This resplendent apparition wasn't just a chance visitor, then; he was actually going to work on roundup.

Weary, sitting cross-legged in the shade of a wagon wheel, glanced up at Pink fumbling shyly among the knives and forks, and then down again at his plate. Thoughtfully he mopped rich brown gravy up with half a biscuit, and absently whistled under his breath:

39

"Oh, tell me, pretty maiden,
Are there any more at home like you? . . ."

—that being the latest song hit.

Pink glanced at him quickly, then at the solemn faces of the others, and retreated hastily inside the cook-tent. Even Happy Jack and Slim saw that the little dude had caught Weary's meaning all right. But they only lowered eyelids at one another and said nothing.

With a heaped plate and brimming cup, Pink retired diffidently to the farthest bit of shade he could find, which, brought him close to Cal Emmett. He sat down gingerly, trying not to spill anything; but in spite of his efforts he splashed coffee on his tan shoes, which plainly distressed him.

Cal gave him a round-eyed, baby stare. "Going to work for the outfit?" he inquired politely.

"Yes sir," Pink answered diffidently in his soft treble. "The overseer gave me a position herding cattle. I just came to town this morning. Is it hard work?"

"Gee whiz, yes!" Cal shook his head disconsolately. "What with taming wild broncos and trying to keep the cattle from stampeding, a busy bee sure has got nothing on us when it comes to improving each shining hour." He bit largely into a biscuit. "Yes sir, it's a hard, hard life." He sighed deeply and drained his cup of coffee.

"My! I always thought I'd like the life of a cowboy," Pink ventured hesitantly.

Cal gave him another round, unwinking stare. "That's because you've been reading books. I read one once,

40

about the cowboy life. The feller that wrote it sure made it sound pretty, all right, but it ain't that way in real life. You won't like it—nobody does. I never heard of anybody liking the life of a cowboy!"

Pink looked up from sawing his knife through a slab of beefsteak. "Why don't you give it up, then, and get a position at something else you do like?"

"Can't." Cal shot furtive glances to right and left, and spoke behind his hand. "We're most of us escaped desperadoes with a price on our heads." He shook his head bodefully. "Workin' as cowboys, see, gives us horses to ride. And we get to know the country. That makes it easy in case a posse was to show up. We could always make a getaway."

"Yes, I guess that's so," Pink murmured.

"Feller that's an outlaw," Cal further unbosomed himself, "he keeps his eyes peeled. Any suspicious stranger comes ridin' into camp, he just saddles a good fast horse and splits the breeze wide open gittin' away from there." He chewed and swallowed the last of his biscuit. "No sir, it's an awful handy job for outlaws. They can work and earn money whilst they're on the dodge."

"I see." Pink's eyes looked like a frightened child's. "Do you mean that—I don't want to be personal—but—that is, are you—?"

"An outlaw?" Cal kindly assisted him. He looked carefully around him. "Don't ever come up behind me sudden, or lay a hand on me in the dark," he warned Pink under his breath. "A hunted man is liable to shoot first and ask questions afterwards. And there's a sheriff in South Dakota, and Texas Rangers in Texas, that's swore

41

to take me in. They'll never git me alive, though—I'll give yuh my oath on that!"

Pink looked distressed. "I'm awfully sorry," he said timidly. "I hope they don't find out where you are working on the dodge."

Cal wagged his head and tried to look discouraged. "A man's luck will hold just so long and no longer," he declared bitterly. "I can stave off the evil hour but someday it's bound to overtake me. I'll git my invite to a necktie party sooner or later. There ain't no escape."

"I've been to necktie parties. Last winter." Pink nodded complete understanding. "I sure do hope I can escape any more. You always get the wrong girl."

"What I'm afraid of," Cal gloomed, "is that I'll get the wrong kind of necktie. You ever been at a lynching bee?"

Pink shook his head. "I—I don't think so. Only spelling bees. Excuse me—I think the overseer is motioning for me."

He hurried over to where Chip was standing alone and asked if he should change clothes and get ready to work that afternoon.

"That was the general idea when I hired you," Chip said in his ironical way. "How did you make out with the boys?"

"They're nice," Pink told him evasively, and picked up his suitcase and another bulky bundle which Chip had unpacked from the extra horse, and took them into the bed-tent Chip had indicated with a wave of the hand.

Weary, having tossed his plate and cup into the dishtub, sauntered over to where Chip stood rolling a smoke. "Where did you pluck that modest flower, Chip?"

Chip sifted some tobacco into the little paper trough in his fingers. "I picked it in town," he said. "I hired it to punch cows. And its botanical name is wait a minute . . ." He put away the tobacco sack, finished his cigarette, placed it between his lips and got out his little book and turned the leaves while the Happy Family crowded around him. "Here it is. Its name is Percival Cadwallader Perkins."

"Oh, mamma! Percival Cadwolloper—*what?*" Weary gazed blankly around the group. "On the dead, Chip, did you make that up?"

"Not on your life! My wildest imagination wouldn't fly that high. That's the name, boys. Percival Cadwallader Perkins."

"Percival Cadwolloper Perkins." Weary whispered the words, savoring each one. "You want to double the guard tonight, Chip. That name sure will stampede the herd."

"He sure is a sweet young thing. Mamma's precious little lamb broke out of the home corral," Cal Emmett offered. "What'll you bet a tall, yellow-haired mamma with flowing widow's weeds won't be out here hunting her runaway offspring inside a week?"

Weary laughed gently. *"Mamma had a little lamb,"* he began to extemporize, *"Its cheeks were red and rosy. And everywhere that mamma went . . ."*

"That lamb was sure to mosey!" Happy Jack surprisingly contributed.

"No, by golly! You got that all hindside before," Slim

43

made loud objection. *"Everywhere that lambie went, his mamma was sure to mosey!"*

Further poetical flights were prevented by the reappearance of Pink. If he had looked pretty in his town clothes, in cowboy garb he was almost too beautiful. The Happy Family gazed at him and drew long breaths of admiration. When his back was turned they shaded their eyes and squinted as if dazzled by his splendor.

Pink still wore his pink-and-white-striped silk shirt, his gray trousers and russet leather belt with silver buckle. But around his neck, nestling under his dimpled chin, was a gorgeous rose-pink neckerchief of the shade he always wore, and which had given him the nickname of Pink.

His hands were hidden in a pair of wonderful silk-embroidered buckskin gauntlets. His trousers were tucked into number-five tan riding boots, high as to heel—so high that they looked two sizes smaller than they were—with silk-stitched tops. A shiny new pair of silver-mounted spurs jingled from his heels. And topping all, a pearl-gray Stetson sat jauntily on his golden curls.

He smiled sweetly at Chip, showing his dimples, which were not lost upon the Happy Family. And he leaned with a studiously graceful pose against the high wheel of the mess wagon and got out a brand new sack of Bull Durham and book of wheatstraw papers. Inwardly he was afraid he might give himself away to the Happy Family, whose fame had spread abroad and whom he felt honor-bound to deceive. But he had to risk it, for he was famished for a smoke.

"Get onto the way he rolls 'em—backwards!" Weary murmured into Cal Emmett's ear.

"If there's anything I hate," Cal observed to the crew, "it's to see a girl chewing a tutti-frutti cud—or smoking a cigarette!"

Pink looked up from under his thick brown lashes and opened his lips to speak, then decided against it. They were pretty sharp, all of them. If he laid it on too thick, they'd be likely to get wise to him. So he merely permitted the wind to blow out three matches for him before he finally got his cigarette lighted, and turned to watch the horse wrangler and two or three of the boys corral the cavy as they came jingling into camp for the noon change of saddle horses.

To Pink their jingling bells were the sweetest music he had heard for many a long, lonesome day. Back there in Minnesota he had dreamed of hearing the bells as the saddle bunch was driven into camp, and now the reality set his blood tingling.

"Weary, you and Cal better relieve the boys on herd," Chip called out, shaking out his loop as he walked toward the corral. He looked at Pink. "I'll get you a horse, Perkins, and you can go along. Then tonight your go on guard with Weary, here."

"Yes, sir," said Pink, and followed Chip out to the corral where Cal and Weary were roping their horses.

Chip presently led out a gentle little cow-pony that could almost take care of a day herd without a rider, and Pink awkwardly bridled him before the covertly watching crew. With his tongue between his teeth he managed to pin one ear of the pony down flat with the headstall. He also managed to blush and to act very much confused when he discovered his blunder. And when he caught the look in Weary's eyes he felt that his reputation as a tender young lad from the East was practically impregnable.

A new saddle, stiff and unbroken to the back of a horse, requires time and considerable language in its proper adjustment. Pink omitted the language—in which he was most proficient—and for that reason, perhaps, the process of saddling the pony took longer than any cowboy would have believed possible. But Cal and Weary smoked and waited with an air of superhuman endurance. When Pink finally boosted himself into the saddle with the aid of both horn and cantle, they rode away to the herd, not daring to look at each other.

Pink ran a quick appraising eye over the twelve hundred range-fattened steers that grazed quietly on a side-hill half a mile or more from camp. Within fifty head he estimated their number correctly, and gloried silently in their splendid condition.

Cal Emmett, close beside him, misinterpreted the glance. "Never saw so many cattle in one bunch before, I bet!"

Pink shook his head vaguely, not taking his wondering gaze off the herd.

"Does one man own all those cows?" he asked with the eager incredulity of a child.

"And then some. This ain't any herd at all; this is just a few culls they're shippin' to get 'em outa the way of the real herd."

"Oh." Pink's tone accepted that bold statement without

question. "About how many do you think there are here?"

Cal winked at Weary and turned his back upon his conscience. "Oh, there's only six thousand, seven hundred and twenty here," he lied boldly. "Last bunch we gathered was fifty-one thousand, twenty-nine and a half."

Pink glanced bewilderedly from one to the other. "You mean—a half a cow? I don't see—"

Cal laughed indulgently. "Oh, the half was a calf that got in by mistake—I caught it afterwards and took it back to its mother."

"I should think that would be pretty hard to do. That's an awful lot of cows to pick out the right mother from."

Cal slid sidewise in the saddle. "Well," he said gravely, "a calf is always like its mother, hair for hair. This calf had white hind feet, one white ear and the deuce of diamonds on its left side. All I had to do was ride the range till I found the cow that matched."

"Oh!" Pink looked deeply impressed.

Weary, smiling to himself, rode off to take his station at the other side of the herd. Pink showed an inclination to follow.

"You stay where you're at, sonny," Cal told him over his shoulder, as he started in the other direction.

"What shall I do?"

Cal's voice came back to him faintly: "Just dub around quiet, and don't bother the cattle."

"And darned good advice, even if it did come from him," Pink muttered, looking after him. So he prepared for a lazy afternoon in the saddle and he expected to enjoy every minute of it.

CHAPTER SIX

W<small>HEN THE</small> three were relieved at suppertime, Pink rode back to camp between Cal and Weary, looking as if he had something on his mind.

"Anything bothering you, Cadwolloper?" Weary asked solicitously.

Pink's eyes flew open at the name; then he swallowed and let it pass. "I'd like to ask Mr. Cal," he began timidly, "how you fed that calf before you found its mother. Didn't he get pretty hungry?"

"Why, I carried a bottle of milk with me," Cal lied fluently. "That calf sure had a big appetite When the bottle got empty I had to catch a cow and milk it."

"Back home," Pink offered, "you always tie a cow in the shed before you milk it; or most always. A real gentle one will stand all right if it has a bucket of mash. Out here on the prairie I don't see how—"

"Cowboys," Cal declared, "have to learn the ways of cow-brutes. Just a secret of the range. A wild range cow will gentle right down if you know the right way to approach 'em. There's certain kinds of sounds you have to make that they understand."

"I'd like to learn them," Pink said eagerly. "I'm going to be a cowboy, so I ought to know how to catch a cow and milk it, hadn't I?" He looked from one to the other. "What kind of sounds do you make?"

He had Cal there. Telling tall stories is one thing, but there was a well-defined limit to Cal's powers of invention. "That's a range secret," he hedged lamely. "It wouldn't do for everybody to know it, or range calves would die of starvation—'cause folks would always be stealing milk from their mothers. No," he added firmly, "you have to be a cowboy for a year before you can learn the secret."

"Oh, excuse me. I didn't mean to be too inquisitive. But about the calf—how did you carry it, Mr. Cal? In your arms, or—"

"The calf? Sure, I carried it in my arms." Cal's big baby-blue eyes matched Pink's for innocence. "I carried that bossy for three days in my arms," he declared solemnly, "before I found a cow with white hind feet, one white ear and the deuce of clubs—"

"Diamonds," Pink corrected.

"Yeah. Sure. Diamonds on its right hind—er—shoulder—"

"The calf's was on its left side," Pink said reproachfully. "Maybe you didn't find the right mother after all."

"Sure I did!" Cal contended earnestly. "She was so grateful when she seen me heave in sight over a hill a mile away she come up on the dead gallop a-bawling. And when I set the calf down beside her she turned her head around and licked my hand!"

Pink drew a long, appreciative sigh. "Cowboy life certainly is interesting," he declared with feeling. And since the discussion had carried them into camp, the conversation was dropped.

Pink dismounted stiffly and walked wide to the cooktent. He was not putting on, either. Ten months away from a horse, with a new, unbroken saddle to begin on again, took its toll even of his hardy young muscles. He

49

didn't have to be an actor to show himself a mighty uncomfortable young man.

He ate hungrily and in silence, unrolled his new bed in a shady spot which Chip had indicated with a nod of the head, and lay down with not a thought for the part he was playing. Such remarks as he overheard from the Flying U boys he passed over with absolute indifference. His face felt burned with the wind and sun, and his muscles ached from that new saddle. He heard Weary remark, just around the corner of the bed-tent out of sight, that Cadwolloper was about all in, and that day herding was too strenuous for him; but he only wondered sleepily where in the world Weary had gotten hold of that Cadwolloper name.

The last he heard, someone was chanting enthusiastically:

"Mamma had a precious lamb,
Its cheeks were red and rosy;
And when he rode the festive bronc,
He tumbled on his nosey!"

There was more, but Pink had gone to sleep and so missed it.

Such is the momentum of long habit that at sundown he awoke with the jingling of the cavy bells and went out to saddle the night horse which Chip caught for him— keeping up the pretense that he was a tenderfoot. And as soon as the horse was tied safely to a wheel of the mess wagon, Pink went back to bed. When he was shaken gently and told it was time for the middle guard, he yawned and dressed with practiced speed, adding a pair of white Angora chaps before he ambled out to where he had left his horse.

Guided and coached by Weary, he took his station at the herd and began that monotonous round which had long been a part of the life he loved best. The beef herd had grazed comfortably until sundown and had been eased onto the bed-ground which was now familiar to them. Only a few restless animals here and there were on their feet; and these, when Pink rode past, were placidly chewing their cuds and would soon lie down to sleep. The moon shone brightly at intervals, with patches of silvery clouds racing before the wind and casting black shadows in splashes over the sleeping land. Standing night guard on such a peaceful night, with the cattle so contented, was largely a matter of form; mostly a precaution against unforeseen events—such as an old-time joke played upon a tenderfoot.

Weary, Pink noticed, seemed very uneasy, and continually stared off toward camp as if expecting someone. Pink would have preferred to stand his shift quietly and without incident, but when Weary's anxiety became so pronounced that a blind man would have noticed it, he felt that he really should rise to the bait and find out what was brewing. So when they met on the far side of the herd, he pulled up awkwardly and asked Weary if he didn't feel well.

Weary leaned and peered into Pink's face. "What makes you ask me that?" he demanded gloomily. "Is it sticking out all over me?"

"Well," Pink hesitated. "I just thought you were worried about something, and I wondered if there was any-thing I could do to help."

Weary shook his head, then stood in the stirrups to peer toward town. "Most generally," he said, "I carry my troubles locked in my own breast. But there's times when a man needs a friend." He studied Pink, sighed and looked away.

"I'd like to be a friend, Mr. Weary," Pink ventured, his eyes big and childlike in their innocence.

Weary reined around and rode beside him. "You're so young," he mused aloud, "and so inexperienced. You don't know how hard and cruel the world can be."

"Oh, yes I do," Pink expostulated earnestly. "I've had troubles with the world myself, Mr. Weary."

"Not real ones. Not old he-man troubles."

Emboldened by his earnestness, Pink rashly forged ahead. "I've been in jail," he said bitterly. "All night, too. I didn't do what they thought I had, but they locked me up just the same. I guess I know a little something about how hard the world can be."

Weary looked at him long in the moonlight. "Mr. Perkins, you give me the courage to trust you. I never did what I'm accused of doing, either. But I'm a hunted man just the same. Ride over here a little ways from the cattle while I tell you. Perkins, I've got an awful foreboding. I dreamed a posse had caught me and was going to string me up to pay for another man's misdeeds. Dreams like that," Weary solemnly declared, "don't come for nothing. It was a warning."

"Maybe," Pink hazarded hopefully, "it was the beans. They tasted kinda sour to me."

"No sir. I've got a feeling they're coming for me tonight." Weary looked fearfully around him, at the sleeping cattle and the quiet moonlit prairie. The roundup camp was a vague splotch of grayish white away over by the creek.

"If I could just get an hour's start—" Weary looked piteously at Pink—"maybe I could get a witness that would prove my innocence. But if they find me now—" His voice dropped to a hollow note of despair.

"Is there anything I could do, Mr. Weary?" Pink's voice quavered a little. "If there's anything I could do or say to them—"

Hope sprang into Weary's face. He leaned over and laid a hand on the neck of Pink's gentle horse. "Mr. Perkins, if you could hold them here—or if I just had a horse that could get out and drift—"

Pink thought he caught the meaning. "Is—do you think my horse would be any good, Mr. Weary?" he asked eagerly. "If he will, you can take him. I'll stay here and—and fool them as long as I can. I could engage them in conversation—"

Weary gazed deeply into Pink's eyes. "Perkins, you're a friend in need. If you'd change horses with me—if they come, I could make a run for it. This horse looks good, but what I need is a stayer. How can I thank you?"

Voices and a faint thudding of galloping hoofs came faintly to their ears. "It's them!" Weary said, and dismounted. "Perkins, I'll never forget you for this. Stall 'em off as long as you can—make 'em think you're the man they want. They won't hang you—there's men there that know me by sight, and the minute they lay

53

hands on you and drag you off your horse, they'll know you ain't me. Maybe, Perkins, we'll meet again and I can thank you proper."

And with that he mounted Pink's horse and rode off at a walk, lying low over the neck of the horse.

Changing horses had not been a part of Weary's plan, and when he looked back over his shoulder and saw Percival Cadwallader Perkins standing there by Glory, holding the bridle-reins and watching him go, his conscience smote him. But it was too late now to change his mind. The boys were coming.

One thing bothered him. He couldn't understand why Chip had played off ignorant of the whole scheme, going to bed early like that and beginning to snore gently almost before his head struck the pillow. But of course, Chip's duty as roundup foreman wouldn't let him openly approve a bit of hazing, however much he might like to be in on the fun. Shutting his eyes to what went on was about the best he could do, and Weary decided that Chip was playing along with them unofficially, and he certainly appreciated it.

As had been planned, he rode down into a grassy draw out of sight and turned short toward the make-believe posse, the idea being to join it before it reached Pink, and miss none of the fun. He would have to hang back and not join in the loud talk and threats of hanging, because Mamma's little lamb might possibly recognize his voice. But he meant to see the fun, anyway.

Pink, playing his part, mounted Glory, and as the posse came in sight, he started riding toward them. Then, when he was certain they had seen him, he wheeled and galloped away across the flat, ostensibly trying to lead them off Weary's trail. That was exactly what they had hoped he would do. On such a lovely clear night, and with the cattle so quiet and all, they expected to give the kid quite a lot of excitement before they let him go.

With their neckerchiefs tied across their noses, they were sure he wouldn't recognize them at all. They would simply let him talk them out of hanging him, and ride off to find Weary; and Weary would steal back to the herd, thank Pink for his help and be extra nice to him afterwards to make up for it. So, with Pink bouncing in the saddle of the easiest-riding horse in the country—when he chose to be easy—the posse yelled blood-curdlingly (though not too loud) and gave chase.

After that the scheme somehow blew up. Happy Jack, not having a night horse saddled, had borrowed one not remarkable for its surefootedness. No sooner had they started full tilt after Pink than Happy Jack's horse stepped in a hole and turned a half somersault which was bad enough to begin with—but when he got up he planted a foot on Jack's diaphragm and then bolted. They thought he had killed Happy Jack and stopped their devilment right there, dismounting beside the fallen man who did not move. It was a sorry end to their joke—or they thought so for a few minutes, until Happy Jack got the breath back into his lungs.

With stirrups snapping like pistol shots, Happy's horse tore down through the dreaming cattle; and, to use a range phrase, the beef herd "jumped the bed-ground and quit the earth," with no one at hand to check the stampede, even if that had been possible.

When Jack came up sputtering sand and profane language, and the boys remembered they were supposed to be a posse, there was no herd; and no Percival Cadwallader Perkins was anywhere in that portion of the country.

Weary burst into the nearly empty bed-tent and got Chip by the shoulder, shaking him none too gently. "Chip! We—we've lost Cadwolloper!" His voice was tragic.

"Hell!" snapped Chip, lying down again. "Don't let that worry you."

"But we've lost the herd, too," Weary added dismally. Whereupon Chip came up clawing for his boots.

They searched for the rest of that night, with a malicious moon drawing veils of clouds before its face to hamper them further with darkness. Dawn brought them to the edge of a coulee, and they looked down and saw their beef herd quietly grazing there, one lone rider on a bright sorrel horse standing guard.

"Mamma!" gasped Weary. "Now, how do you suppose Cadwolloper got this far from camp?"

A shamefaced Happy Family galloped down the hill and headed for Pink, who rode to meet them looking not in the least like a cherub.

"You knock-kneed bunch of locoed sheepherders," he greeted them in high dudgeon, "it's about time you showed up! If you think you can hold this herd for an hour, I'll go to camp. I doubt if you can. I'd hate to bet you could hold a bunch of sick lambs inside a corral with the gate locked on the outside.

"You long-eared smart alecks, you couldn't earn your

56

board on a ten-acre farm in Minnesota, driving one milk cow and a yearling calf to pasture and back! Up on Milk River, they'd put bells on every darn one of you to keep you from getting lost going from the mess house to the corral and back!" He eased his saddle-galled person over to one side in the saddle, and singled out Weary for his next volley of wrath.

"And by the way, I've heard a lot about this sorrel skate you call Glory. Word came up to the Cross L that he was quite a horse. I will say he's the biggest disappointment I've met up with in many a long day.

"Next time you give a man a horse you want him to fall off of, for the Lord's sake don't put him on a gentle old pelter that would be duck soup for a two-year-old. I'm sick and tired of trying to delude myself into thinking that this thing I've got under me is a horse."

Then, as quickly as it had flared up, his anger died. He looked at the Happy Family pulled up ten paces before him, staring slack-jawed, and his dimples showed. Laughter spilled into his eyes and his voice. He kicked Glory forward and held out his gaudily gauntleted hand to Weary.

"Next time you frame a greenhorn," he bantered gleefully, "make damn sure it ain't Milk River Pink."

A stunned silence held until Weary found voice enough to say, with his whimsical drawl, "Cadwolloper, the drinks are on us!" And he added, as the Happy Family gathered round to shake Pink by the hand, "I'd rather be sold out by Milk River Pink than anybody I know!"

CHAPTER SEVEN

BEEF ROUNDUP was over; spring calves had been gathered and weaned. The first snowstorm of the season had swished over the rangeland for a day and a night with a threat of real winter, only to be routed by a warm southwest wind which turned the snow into six inches of slush which the horses' feet churned into mud along the unfrozen road. Even the mud had dried weeks ago and the lumps and rough edges of the ruts had been pulverized into dust again. Winter was holding off for a long spell of Indian summer.

Those warm, smoky days when the nights were nippy and white frost lay in the shady spots until the warm sun of midday searched them out made life worth living. But they were busy days, too. The Flying U roundup wagons had been brought in under the shed and their canvas tops folded away in the harness room until the green grass showed in the spring. The crew of fifteen riders had been cut down to the six who called Flying U Coulee home— six without counting Chip Bennett, who ate and slept in the White House, as befitted the foreman and brother-in-law of the Old Man, but who spent most of his waking hours with the Happy Family. But six nevertheless, now that Pink was a member in good standing.

What with wood and coal to haul, fences to mend, stables and sheds to bank and tighten against the fine-sifting snow and bitter winds; with the roundup horses to be thrown on winter range and watched for a while until they were located there, and a multitude of small chores and preparations for winter, the Flying U boys scarcely marked the passing of time, it went so quickly.

And now, here it was Thanksgiving Eve, and the big dance in the Dry Lake schoolhouse was in full swing and had been for a good three hours. The floor manager had just called out that it was ladies' choice; and Weary, leaning against the wall near the door, was watching the amorous torment Happy Jack was experiencing as the thin, expressionless face of Annie Pilgreen swung towards him with secret purpose in her pale-blue eyes. Which one of the two was the homelier or the more bashful, Weary couldn't decide, but it occurred to him that if beauty is a magnet, the lack of it seems to have as strong a power of attraction for its kind.

Weary found it good as a show to watch those two. Annie was going to make Happy Jack her ladies' choice, all right, and Happy Jack had his eyes glued on her in a rapturous kind of apprehension, wanting and yet dreading to have her single him out for her partner. As she approached with a vague indirectness that could fool no one, Happy sidled skittishly toward the door. Unless Weary headed him off, Annie would need to hit a faster pace if she caught him before he broke out through the door and stampeded into the night.

Weary was so interested in the little drama that he completely forgot the possibility of feminine designs upon himself. When a small hand was laid with a gentle firmness upon his arm, he jumped and whirled that way as if someone had slapped him in the face.

The hand belonged to the schoolma'am who taught at the Meeker schoolhouse. Her name was Ruby Satterlee, and the few times Weary had met her she had looked at him as if he were still reprehensibly engaged in tying a drunken, protesting old man on a skittish horse—which made him wary of chance meetings.

Tonight, however, a new and strange gleam was in her long-lashed brown eyes, but she was smiling, evidently wanting to be friendly; and having learned by observation that the schoolma'am was a swell dancer, Weary surrendered and took a step toward the dance floor where couples were already stepping off the Rye waltz.

"I'd rather sit this one out, Mr. Davidson, if you don't mind," the schoolma'am murmured as close to his ear as her sixty inches of height would permit. "Let's go over there in the corner by the music, and sit down where we can talk."

"Why, certainly," Weary assented politely, hoping he did not look as uncomfortable as he felt.

As they made their way around the edge of the room, certain vague impressions gained that evening fused into a coherent pattern, though what it signified he could not imagine just then. To put it plainly, the schoolma'am had been sitting out an astonishing number of dances that night, and always with a different partner.

It occurred to Weary now that several of the Flying U boys had sat beside her at one time or another, and that the schoolma'am had seemed to have a lot to talk about. He didn't much like it, but she had roped him for fair, and he didn't see how he was going to break away. It did not help him, either, to remember how every partner she had talked to confidentially during a dance had looked worried when he left her.

For perhaps three minutes Weary sat with his head bent in a listening attitude, while a hunted look crept into his own eyes. "But Miss Satterlee, *I* can't act," he protested earnestly during her first pause.

"Oh, yes, you could if you tried," the schoolma'am corrected him with sweet assurance difficult to resist. "It's really nothing alarming that I have in mind; just a good old-fashioned Christmas entertainment in the schoolhouse, with a tree for the youngsters—well, and the grownups too, I suppose. I never saw the human being yet that didn't simply adore getting a present off a Christmas tree; did you?"

"They wouldn't," Weary stated with dark meaning, "if they had to sit and listen to me speak a piece first. They'd likely let the Christmas tree wait while they had a good old-fashioned lynching bee."

Miss Satterlee laughed. "I wouldn't risk your neck for the world; I'm sure you're much too valuable a factor in the community to be snuffed out like that. Why, who would think of all those boomerang jokes if they hung you, Mr. Davidson?" She gave another little laugh, glanced up sidelong into Weary's reddening face and returned to her real purpose.

"An entertainment doesn't necessarily mean that everyone must stand up and recite poetry," she said in a soothing tone. "I only ask you to promise me you'll help. Getting up an entertainment that will be really entertaining means a lot of work, you know. Surely that district out there doesn't expect the schoolma'am to do everything, and they just sit there like lunks, enjoying the show!"

She was tapping one foot in time to the music. In time with her impatience, too, Weary thought as he looked down at her. Her eyes were beginning to sparkle and he thought in a minute or two they would begin snapping with indignation. And though she was asking something beyond all reason, he didn't want to make her mad. He thought it was a pretty good time to start crawfishing.

"I sure would like to help you out, Miss Satterlee," he told her in his pleasantest drawl, "but the fact is, I don't expect to be here along about Christmas time. It's about the only time I can get off, and I've got to have some teeth filled—"

The schoolma'am's foot beat double time. "You're the fourth Flying U man who has to get his teeth filled at Christmas time," she interrupted him. "Why don't you club together and have a dentist come down to the ranch? Or were you expecting to fill your teeth with turkey?"

That was too much for Weary. He sighed, and raised both hands unobtrusively in surrender. "Well, if I'm here I'm sure willing to help," he said. "I could tend to the curtain for you—if you had a curtain."

"I really don't aspire to more than one curtain," the schoolma'am said sweetly, "and seven brawny young men have spoken for the job of pulling the curtain. I'm afraid, Mr. Davidson, I can only promise to bear you in mind, in case there is a vacancy."

Her sarcasm was a fearful thing to face, though it delighted him, too. Weary grinned and resorted to wheedling. "Do you *have* to go to all the trouble and bother of getting up a program?" he murmured.

"Couldn't we just have a nice big tree, lots of candy and presents for all the kids? Nobody wants to sit and have the Night-before-Christmas-and-all-through-the-house fired at them when they're busy wondering what Santy brought 'em. That's just plain tantalizing.

"I'll work like a dog to help rig up the biggest, finest tree the Meeker schoolhouse will hold—but being put in an entertainment program is something I have to draw the line at. Call it off, why don't you? You could work and slave to train a bunch of kids to speak pieces, and what thanks would you get? I'd give up the idea, if I was you, Miss Satterlee."

The schoolma'am looked up at him through the longest, thickest, curliest lashes in the world, it seemed to Weary. "I've already promised the children that we would have an entertainment and a Christmas tree—and when a schoolteacher promises anything to a roomful of children, nothing short of death or smallpox would be considered an excuse for failing to keep that promise; and I have just ten tongue-tied kids to work with!"

Whether she did it deliberately or not, the way she suddenly abandoned schoolteacher talk and dropped into an everyday tone and speech affected Weary more deeply than any argument she could have brought forth. She could have stopped talking right there, for his resistance was melting like a washboiler full of snow set on a hot kitchen stove. She went on:

"Of course, when I promised that, I thought all the young folks of the neighborhood would help. I thought they were all my friends. But now I have begun to call the roll, I don't seem to have any friends in the district."

Her voice trembled a little when she said that, and her slipper toe stopped tapping the floor and dodged back out of sight under her blue silk skirt.

Weary surprised himself by an impulse to reach out and pat her hand, which was an incredible thing for him to want to do to any girl.

"Oh, you don't want to feel that way about it, Miss Satterlee. You've got the wrong idea about us. I guess you don't know it, but all us cowboys, we're shy. I don't mean bashful, like Happy Jack over there—he's bashful like hay fever; it comes on sudden and violent when he sees a girl. What I mean, we're modest and retiring. We shun the public eye. We hate to do anything that would make us conspicuous—"

"Such as kidnaping a poor, feeble old man in broad daylight on the main street of town, and leading him off tied on a horse?" The schoolma'am's eyes, Weary thought, looked even more innocent than Cadwolloper when he was up to some devilment. "Or taking a great lot of can openers to a roundup cook to cure his acute indigestion?"

"Mamma!" exclaimed Weary under his breath, forgetting where he was.

" 'Mamma' certainly wouldn't approve of such goings-on," the schoolma'am said with an irrepressible giggle. "So you see, Mr. Davidson, you can't pull the wool over my eyes a little bit. I consider you a very talented young man. Your histrionic ability fairly scintillates; when you least expect to be, you're highly entertaining."

"I wish you'd spell those two words for me, Miss Satterlee," Weary requested with specious humility. "I'll have to look them up in the dictionary. I can't just read their brand by sight."

"Histrionic and scintillating? You needn't bother with the dictionary, Mr. Davidson. I never use words unless I know their meaning, so I'll tell you and save you time and trouble. Histrionic means acting—on the stage, technically. Scintillate means to shine; sparkle; dazzle."

Weary caught a grin just in time and pinched it into the corners of his mouth. "Mamma! Do you mean, Miss Satterlee, I really do sparkle and dazzle? I'll have to tell the boys that. I never did think they appreciated me enough."

The schoolma'am gave him a quick glance of suspicion, but Weary's face could be very misleading upon occasion. Just now it was grave and his eyes showed a real concern over his defects.

"You certainly can put on a show when you want to," she retorted briskly. "I wouldn't say you are exactly dazzling, however. But let's not get away from the real issue. Are you or aren't you willing to give me some little assistance this next month, in trying to make my Christmas entertainment and tree a success?"

"We-ell, if I don't have to go up to Great Falls to the dentist—or—"

"Of course, I don't want to appeal to your sympathy, or even your humanity or sense of fair play," she cut short his temporizing in the swift, devastating way she had. "The mere fact that this is my first attempt to teach school, and that I am an orphan and have no home, and unless I make a go of schoolteaching I shall probably have to wash dishes in somebody's kitchen, has no bearing whatever on the subject. Nor has the mere detail that I am trying to put my kid brother through school with my salary, so that he can begin to earn money and help support me in my old age.

"All these things need not be considered in the matter. But I did want to make a success of this school business, so that the board of directors will hire me again and I can be sure of getting Johnny graduated and into some business. That is not your concern, of course. All in the world I am asking of you, Mr. Davidson, is whether you're willing to help me a little with this entertainment."

It was quite a long speech but it flowed out swiftly while the crowd on the dance floor was stepping off:

If a body meet a body comin' through the rye,
If a body kiss a body, need a body cry?

The schoolma'am's words reminded Weary of molten lead poured into bullet molds. They chilled swiftly into the hard pattern of her life and formed a picture he must carry with him always. A gritty little girl of about twenty, smart as a whip and full of fun if she had a chance to be, starting out to make her own way in the world with a lunk of a brother on her back.

In the space of one breath Weary knew a keen desire to find that brother and back him up in a corner and talk turkey to him for a few minutes. Hell, if he was big enough to graduate from school, he was big enough to hold down a job and work his way through. What kind of a spineless lout was he, anyway? Look at Abraham

Lincoln—look at himself: He'd worked his way through all of school except college, and made it before he was seventeen. This little schoolma'am . . .

He laid a finger on her arm. "Don't fire the other barrel, I'm running on three legs now! What I mean, I'll do anything you want me to—anything I *can* do."

"Thank you. I knew you would." The schoolma'am promptly drew a little memorandum' book from some hidden pocket, opened it to a page which had six or eight other names neatly written down, and added Will Davidson to the list.

And to himself Weary said, "Stung!" But all the same he liked it.

CHAPTER EIGHT

APPARENTLY THE schoolma'am believed in striking while the iron was hot. On the second day after the Thanksgiving dance, Weary, returning from an errand to Dry Lake, met Joe Meeker up on the bench above Flying U Coulee. Joe had a message for the Flying U outfit, and he was glad to pass it on to Weary and hurry back home; for a cold north wind was blowing, and riding against it was no pleasure.

Weary mulled the message, and all it portended, in his mind all the way down the hill and while he was putting away his horse and doing his share of the chores. It made him shiver just to think of taking active part in an entertainment. But fresh angles and new possibilities kept coming into his mind, and by the time the Happy Family was gathered in the bunkhouse to clean up for supper,

Weary had decided the matter for the whole outfit. All that remained was to convince the boys that it was settled—and Weary prided himself on being a very convincing fellow.

"Schoolma'am wants us all to go over to the schoolhouse tonight, and be there at seven-thirty sharp," he began casually. "We're supposed to help make medicine over the Christmas entertainment business. Slim, she says you've got to be Santa Claus and come down the stovepipe with a bag of toys on your back. She says you've got just the right figure for it." And Weary took his turn at the washbasin, scooping water on his face to hide the expression lurking around his mouth.

The Happy Family looked at one another. Cal Emmett was inspired to burst forth, with more volume than melody:

"Is your name written there
On the page white and fair,
For the school entertainment?
Is your name written there?"

Then he looked around for laughs, and seemed surprised that no one cracked a smile.

As a matter of fact, no one thought it was funny. They had been trying to forget the schoolma'am and her Christmas plan—as their silence on the subject should have told Cal.

"By golly," Slim gulped, "you can just tell the schoolma'am to go to granny! Why don't she ask J. G.? He's a good fifteen pounds fatter than I be."

"You might suggest it tonight," Weary offered. "I told Joe Meeker I'd see you all got there on time, if I had to hogtie the whole bunch of you and haul you over in the hayrack." He dried his face and hands leisurely, and regarded the silent group.

"Oh, mamma, but you're a sour-looking bunch! What's the matter with you boys? Can't you even *look* entertaining?"

"Well, maybe you'll hogtie the whole bunch," Jack Bates observed skeptically, "but if you do, you'll sure be late to meeting, sonny!"

"And you're the feller that's been girl-shy all this time!" Cal grunted. "You got no right to let us in for a thing like that unbeknownst to us."

Weary finished combing his hair before the cracked piece of bar mirror tacked to the wall, and turned to face them. "On the dead, boys, we're in for it, and we might as well take our medicine. I hate it as bad as anybody. Worse, maybe. But I happen to know what's back of it."

"Aw, gwan! That schoolma'am's back of it, that's what! She's got you tied down and branded."

"You're a liar! I've got no use for girls, and you know it. Just because you've been making them goo-goo eyes at Annie you think a fellow has got to fall for a girl in order to think of doing her a favor. I balked on the whole proposition myself, till the schoolma'am up and told me why this entertainment has got to go through."

"Well, why has it?" Pink demanded irritably. "I got tangled up in one of those things back in Minnesota last winter. I swore then it would be the last time, and so help me Josephine, it's going to be!"

"Well, by golly, there ain't going to be any *this* time for me!" Slim declared. "I ain't going within gunshot of that schoolhouse till after Christmas."

"All right, if that's the way you feel about it," Weary told him shortly. "But I happen to know that the schoolma'am is trying her darnedest to make good with the school board. She hasn't got any folks to fall back on—"

"But she has got a kid brother she's trying to put through school somewhere," Pink finished for him.

"Yeah, she like to had me bawlin' like a spanked kid, right there at the dance," Jack Bates said glumly. "She sure knows how to work on a feller's sympathy, battin' them curly eyelashes at him."

Weary looked slightly disconcerted, but he recovered himself. "Well, leave the kid brother out of it, then. It all boils down to the fact that she wants to hold her job and cinch it for next year. And the school kids want an entertainment and tree for Christmas, and she's promised them one.

"That's the schoolma'am's cards, laid on the table. There ain't a thing personal about it. I'd like it better if she was a man. But a job's a job, these days. And me, I'm game to try and help her put it over. Only," he added emphatically, "I draw the line at speaking a piece, and I told her so!"

"Same here," two voices spoke at once.

"What's more, by golly, I draw the line at goin'. She needn't think she can run any rannigan on me, job or no job." Slim pounded his fist on the table to prove that he meant it.

Weary hooked his thumbs inside his belt and let his glance travel slowly from one to the other.

"If you haven't got nerve enough to stay in the game until the deck's shuffled and dealt, you shouldn't have bought a stack of chips."

"Aw—who said—"

"You all promised the schoolma'am you'd help. You sat and let her write your names down in her book. I saw them. Every one of you had your name down ahead of mine. Since when has the Flying U outfit turned out to be quitters?"

"Yeah—that's right," Cal admitted. "Our names are sure written there, on the page white and fair. Looks like it's up to us, boys. What we oughta do is git in there and put the thing through on the run."

"Aw—what you givin' us? Think we're goin'—?"

"Yeah. We'll give 'em a show that'll make their eyes bug out. Happy, you can do a toe dance. All you need is a stirrup hung on a swivel to stick your foot in . . ."

Happy Jack turned a deep purple and grinned in sickly fashion. But before he could think of any bright retort, Jack Bates spoke up.

"Say, Weary, ain't there going to be any female girls in this opry troupe?"

"Sure," Weary answered confidently. "Joe says the Little Doctor promised to help run the show, and Rena Jackson and Len Adams are in it, and Annie Pilgreen." (That last name was purely surmise on Weary's part.) "Her and Happy are down on the program for 'Under the Mistletoe.' Tableau. Red fire, Happy. And you kiss her quick, but keep it lingering till the curtain goes down."

"Aw, gwan! I ain't goin' to do no such a thing!" Happy cried in a tone of deep distress—he not having observed Weary's lowered eyelid.

His violent reaction to the suggestion gave the Happy Family an idea; and an idea, when entertained by that particular group of young men, seldom failed to flower in a huge and elaborate joke upon someone.

"What's Annie think about it, Weary?" Pink wanted to know. "Joe say anything about that?"

"Well, Annie don't believe Happy's got the nerve. You know, boys, it's a shame the way Happy treats that girl; she's crazy about him, and he won't give her a tumble. Of course, she knows he's bashful, but there's a limit to everything. If you ask me, Annie's just about ready to call for a showdown."

"Aw, you're just lyin'! Annie never said no such a thing and I know it!" Beads of perspiration began to show on Happy Jack's forehead.

"Well, all I know is, if I had a girl like Annie, faithful and true—"

"*Aw,* I never said I had a girl!"

"It wouldn't take me more than two minutes to show her I wasn't as scared as I looked."

"Aw, I ain't scared—and I can lick the son-of-a-gun that says I am!"

"All right, then. You show up at the schoolhouse with the rest of the bunch and prove you ain't scared." Weary cocked an ear toward the whanging summons to supper, and joined the rush for the door, pretty well satisfied with the way the boys were swinging into line.

Over at the Meeker schoolhouse that evening, when

Miss Satterlee's little gold watch told her it was seven-thirty, she came out of the corner where she had been whispering with the Little Doctor, and faced a select, anxious-eyed audience. Miss Satterlee was a very direct young person. She went straight to her subject. They all knew what they were there for, she told them.

Although they didn't know but merely feared the worst, the Happy Family looked at her unblinkingly and waited. Cal Emmett's lips were seen to move, saying words over to himself. As a matter of fact, he was seeing if he could remember the only "piece" he knew, just in case he was called upon to recite it. It was one beginning, according to Cal's version:

Twinkle, twinkle, little star,
Where in thunder are you at?

There were thirteen verses and they were not particularly adapted to a Christmas entertainment where women and children might be expected to sit and listen, but Cal had not thought of that angle.

The schoolma'am was explaining in some detail. There would be a tableau, she said (which started the sweat on Happy Jack's face), and Jarley Waxworks.

Cal Emmett left off whispering his star poem and made his eyes round as saucers. "What're them?" he demanded suspiciously.

The schoolma'am gave Cal a pitying look for his ignorance and made careful, somewhat condescending explanation. She began with Charles Dickens, asking how many there had read *The Old Curiosity Shop*. No

73

one had, save the Little Doctor and Len Adams, so the schoolma'am proceeded with a brief sketch of Mrs. Jarley and her Waxworks exhibition which even the youngest Pilgreen child would certainly have understood.

Gradually it dawned upon the Happy Family that they were to be dressed in outlandish costumes and represent wax figures of notorious characters of the past. They would not need to say a word, but would have to stand perfectly still, like statues, until Mrs. Jarley had described them to the audience, and wound them up. When wound up, they would be expected to go through a certain set of motions which were supposed to represent their last act on earth. The schoolma'am added that it was a comedy pantomime and, if properly done, would be very, very funny.

The Happy Family exchanged glances, grinning uncertainly, and the schoolma'am sat down sidewise upon a desk, swung a neat little foot and talked confidentially about the Waxworks, which seemed to be the main feature of the entertainment.

"Mr. Bennett," she said, looking at Chip, "you can be Captain Kidd, the pirate, with long black hair, fierce black mustache and whiskers and a huge curved sword. Mrs. Bennett will kneel at your feet with her hair down her back and tears on her cheeks (we'll manage the tears, Mrs. Bennett, with glass beads fastened on white thread) and a very pitiful expression on her face.

"When your machinery is wound up at the back (we'll use an old alarm clock for that) you, Captain Kidd, will lift your sword and bring it down toward your victim's head, while she leans backward away from the blow, then forward as you raise the sword and backward again as you lower it—do you get the idea?" Her eyes went quickly from face to face, seeking some response. "The idea is that all the motions must be very mechanical and in perfect rhythm—like toys which you wind up to make them go."

The scattering of half-hearted chuckles encouraged her to go on. "Mr. Emmett, we're going to ask you to be Mrs. Jarley and deliver the lectures about the different figures, and wind them up."

Someone snorted over that, and the Happy Family burst into laughter. The worst was over—or so it would seem.

"Mr. Davidson, being the tallest man in the group, will be the Japanese Dwarf, who was a great assassin in his day and who was executed by being made to eat poisoned rice. Mr. Davidson will eat his poisoned rice out of the very largest chopping bowl we can find, with a wooden spoon. A long braided queue made of horsehair, long slim mustache and a large-flowered kimono will be the main features of his costume."

"What are we supposed to use for faces?" Pink asked sweetly. He looked around with his blue eyes innocent. "I don't see how we could keep these straight long enough to look like statues."

"Mrs. Bennett and I have talked that over," the schoolma'am answered pleasantly. "We discussed sending to Great Falls for false faces, but it isn't easy to get masks to fit the characters. In my last year of school we had an entertainment with Jarley Waxworks, and we painted our faces and used false hair.

"As you suggest, Mr. Perkins, it isn't easy to hold a certain expression on the face for any length of time. But we found that if practiced, it could be done." And she dropped a hint of what they might expect. "We found," she said with an odd smile, "that before the rehearsals were over we were all so sick of the whole thing that it was the easiest thing in the world to fix our eyes upon a certain point in space and just look glum."

Cal Emmett, sitting at the end of the row, whispered behind his hand to the others that Happy Jack wouldn't need any rehearsal; all he'd have to do would be to look natural. Certain ones snickered and there was a general tendency to muttered taunts, which shattered the formality of the meeting and turned it into a mild babble of voices offering weird suggestions for the benefit of the other fellow.

Through all the clatter and cross fire of jibes, Happy Jack sat miserably self-conscious in the seat nearest the door and farthest from Annie Pilgreen. The pot-bellied stove yawned red-mouthed at him a scant two feet away; someone coming in chilled with the nipping north wind had shoveled in coal with too lavish a hand, so the stove door had been thrown open as the readiest method of keeping the stove from melting to the floor. Even so, its corpulent middle glowed a bright red, and Happy's wolf-skin overcoat was beginning to smell to high heaven.

"As for the tableau [Happy Jack jumped when he heard that], we can arrange that later, for it will not require any rehearsing. We must get to work on the Wax-works as soon as possible. How soon can you come to rehearse?"

"Every night and all day Sunday," Weary drawled, and the schoolma'am blushed a little and said that twice a week would do.

Having heard the best and the worst, Happy Jack slipped out of the room and went home feeling like a reprieved criminal. The rest of them stayed late at the schoolhouse, and Weary and Pink discussed something enthusiastically in a corner with the Little Doctor and the schoolma'am. The Little Doctor said it was a shame to play tricks on Happy, but both giggled and agreed on a plan. So the Happy Family rode home that night leaning over their saddlehorns in fits of laughter while they talked about Happy Jack.

CHAPTER NINE

THE THIRD rehearsal of the Jarley Waxworks was in progress. Nothing more had as yet been said about the tableau—unless the mysterious whispering in corners had something to do with it. Happy Jack, who was to be the Chinese Giant, was very suspicious of those secret conferences; but so far he had craned his neck and tried to eavesdrop without learning a thing.

The schoolma'am called a ten-minute recess, osten-sibly to let the Waxworks figures relax a bit, but chiefly so that Mrs. Jarley could get the hang of certain long words she had been stumbling over—much to the amusement of her wax figures. Happy Jack stepped off the coal-oil box (and thereby robbed himself miraculously of two feet of stature). The schoolma'am approached him, a look in her eyes that left him shivering. When she laid a finger mysteriously on his arm and drew him into the corner sacred to consultations, Happy Jack's forehead sweated like a stone water jar in hot weather.

"I want to compliment you on the splendid way you hold a pose," she began brightly. "The way you stand up on that box and never move a muscle all the while Mr. Emmett is talking about the others is the finest exhibition of self-control I ever saw. I really don't see how you do it—unless you've had some experience in acting."

Happy Jack swallowed. He wanted to tell her that he was so scared all the time he was petrified, but he couldn't bring himself to put that paralyzing fear into words; and since he couldn't very well tell the schoolma'am to "gwan" he merely grinned and looked ready to die of embarrassment.

"You're so good," Miss Satterlee whispered, "*I must* have you for the tableau I'm planning. The one we'll show the very last thing before Santa Claus jingles his sleigh bells outside."

"Aw, I couldn't act in no tableau," Happy Jack stammered, "I'd just—I'd spoil it. I—you better git somebody else."

"I spoke to Annie Pilgreen about it." The schoolma'am's tone was the one she used to coax a sulky child in the primer class. She was like all the rest, Happy Jack thought. Just because he was homely, she took it for granted he didn't have any brains. And now she was bringing Annie into it. The schoolma'am went on, "I asked her if she was willing to be the one under the mistletoe—she's so fair and delicate-looking she's the very one for it—like some old painting."

The schoolma'am's eyes were measuring every quiver of Happy Jack's face while she talked, and now she hurried on before he could get his mouth open or his courage whipped to the point of refusal. "Annie says she will gladly take part in the tableau, if you have no objections."

Happy Jack's whole being seethed with objections, but he couldn't seem to get any of them out into speech. For one thing, he was in love with Annie, and his love was to him too sacred a thing to be dragged out before everybody, just so they could holler and stomp and whistle. Still, if Annie wanted to be in a tableau with him, Happy would die rather than disappoint her.

On the other hand, he felt as if he would die of heart failure or something if he had to go through with it. He sent a despairing glance at the Happy Family, but they were very much engrossed down by the stage and didn't see him, much less come to the rescue.

He could see Cal Emmett fanning himself with Mrs. Jarley's poppy-trimmed bonnet and trying to recite part of the lecture, hindered more than helped by the prompting of the other boys. Chip was whittling his big curved sword into shape, and Weary had turned the great wooden chopping bowl upside down and was using it for a snare drum, rolling a very skillful tattoo upon it with sticks of kindling wood. Not one of them seemed to remember his existence. They might as well have been a thousand miles away for all the help or comfort he could expect from them.

The schoolma'am drew his attention back to herself with a gentle urgency. "You will do it, won't you? It will only be for a minute, and all you need do is just stand there, bending over Annie as if you meant to— you know. But the curtain will be drawn before anything happens, and the audience is left to guess the rest." She took her hand off his arm with a little laugh. "Then the sleigh bells jingle outside, and Santa Claus comes in."

Happy Jack dragged his tongue back from behind his palate or whatever it was. "Aw, I wouldn't want—"

"I told Annie I was sure you wouldn't mind. I said I could tell just by the way you went after that Chinese Giant part that you were the very one for our closing tableau. She was afraid you would turn down the chance and leave her feeling embarrassed and silly, because she's already agreed to do it."

"Aw, Miss Satterlee, I don't want to hurt Annie's feelings, but—"

"I knew that all the time; so I'll tell her she's had the wrong idea about you and there isn't a thing to worry about. Women are so blind sometimes." The schoolma'am stood up with a competent air as if she had just dismissed a class, but she paused for another word.

"One thing," she said: "you two won't need to rehearse the tableau at all. We'll just place you in position, touch off the red fire and draw the curtain. That's really all there is to it." Then she gave him a bright impersonal smile and went back to marshal the Wax-works into line again.

For Happy Jack the sky had all but fallen. The Wax-works which he had dreaded, the tree, the whole Christmas celebration had dissolved into a blurred night-mare background for that awful tableau. Already he could hear the stomping of feet and the smart-alecky remarks the crowd would yell at him. For all he knew, they would demand an encore just to draw out the agony. Why they had picked on a homely guy like him, he couldn't understand. It wasn't Annie's fault—someone else was at the bottom of it and had put the schoolma'am up to this. Who it was, Happy meant to find out if it took all winter.

Heavily he clumped to his place and mounted the box, thus transforming himself into a Chinese Giant again. His face might have been actually molded in wax, for all the expression it had. But behind it his brain was begin-ning to revolve upon the mystery of his arch-tor-mentor—and when Happy Jack decided to start thinking, he seemed to withdraw from his unprepos-sessing exterior and to brood within the secret fastnesses of his soul.

Other statues might—and did—break into giggles and suppressed laughter, or make remarks not in the book; but the Chinese Giant stood motionless and unaware of what went on around him, his little, deep-set eyes staring straight before him across the blackboard and through it into an unseen world of conjecture.

He didn't really look human. The schoolma'am pointed him out as an example to the others, but he never heard her. Others made facetious comments upon his looks and got no reaction whatever. Even Annie Pilgreen spoke to him and got no answer.

"Happy's swallowed his medicine, all right," the Japanese Dwarf leaned and whispered to Captain Kidd.

Captain Kidd turned and studied the brooding features of the Giant. "He's certainly started the think-works," he muttered to the Dwarf. "It may take him six months or a year to figure the thing out, and see it was a put-up job. But when he does, look out!"

"He can't massacre the whole bunch of us," Weary retorted, "and he'll never know who thought up the idea of that tableau."

"Don't you believe he won't! Happy doesn't think very often, but when he does, he's thorough."

"Here! You statues over there let up on the chin-whackin' or I'll knock some chips off yuh where it won't show!" Mrs. Jarley lifted the stove poker threateningly.

So the Japanese Dwarf returned to his poisoned rice, and Captain Kidd apologized to his victim, and the rehearsal proceeded.

That night Weary rode home beside Happy Jack, who sat humped in the saddle like a calf in its first blizzard. Weary was very sympathetic. He said the Little Doctor had told him about the tableau, but he couldn't see any sense in it. Still, it would only last a minute, and it wouldn't need any rehearsing. "And," he added hearteningly, "it ain't as if you had to kiss her before everybody. The curtain comes down and hides all that."

Happy Jack turned his head then and looked at Weary for what seemed to be a long time. But he didn't say a word; and that should have been warning enough, if Weary had only heeded it.

From that night until Christmas, Happy Jack continued to think. It was not until he was riding gloomily alone on his way to the schoolhouse for the last time, however, that he really saw through the joke. He leaned and slapped his horse affectionately on the neck and grinned for the first time since Thanksgiving night.

"Aw, I betcha that's the way it is, all right, and I betcha . . ." His brain had accelerated to the point where thoughts came thick and fast. He relaxed into a silent cogitation that could scarcely fail to bring results. Then he spurred his horse into a lope, suddenly eager to arrive.

CHAPTER TEN

WEARY, TOO, had cause to do some thinking that evening. At the behest of the schoolma'am, he had made a hurried trip to Dry Lake that day, it having been discovered, when the box of ornaments for the tree had been opened, that the candles had been overlooked.

Five miles out of town where the road started up over the first hill near the head of Gunyon Coulee, he saw a horseman coming down a side road which was a short cut to the Rogers' place. A hundred yards away, the rider hailed him and spurred his horse to a faster pace.

He was a stranger, that was plain to be seen; yet there was a familiar look about him that puzzled Weary; until the young man asked the way to Joe Meeker's place. Then Weary knew.

From the brown eyes and the long thick lashes, the straight dark brows and the shape of the nose, the young man could be none other than the schoolma'am's kid brother. Not such a kid, however, judging by his size and a certain mature look about the eyes. For some inexplicable reason Weary felt a sharp pang of dread—or something very nearly like it.

There was no sense in that, of course. It was perfectly natural that Johnny Satterlee should come to spend Christmas with his sister and take in the doings at the schoolhouse. But for all that, Weary couldn't help making a swift mental calculation of the expense of the trip or thinking that Johnny might better employ his Christmas holiday in work that would bring in a little money to help out.

Furthermore, the schoolma'am hadn't said a word about expecting her brother Johnny; or if she had, no one had mentioned it. It was none of his business, and he told himself so more than once during that ride. But all the same, he couldn't help feeling that the schoolma'am wasn't going to be overly pleased to see Johnny, even if it was Christmas.

When he reached the schoolhouse early that evening he was sure of it. The schoolma'am's cheeks were pink with excitement, but Weary could have sworn that the worried look in her eyes was not caused by any particular anxiety over the success of her program. It seemed as if Fate intended that he should come close to her problem, for he chanced to hear a few words spoken inside the cloakroom just as he was going in after a package left in his overcoat pocket.

The schoolma'am was inside with her brother.

As Weary came to the door he heard Johnny say in a low voice heavy with urgency, "They're all three going to be here, you said. Why don't you get them off to one side, Rue, and tell them you've got to have an advance? They'll give it to you—sure they will, on Christmas."

And Ruby Satterlee answered hurriedly, "But, Johnny, think how it would look! And you haven't even told me why you want it. If you're in some scrape, you'd better tell me—"

"Aw, cut it out," Johnny said irritably. "Can the chatter, can't you, Rue? You'd better get out there and get those old hayseeds together before there's too much of a crowd . . ."

Weary turned back to the tree without his package. He wished he could take that young whelp outside and wring his darned neck for him, but there wasn't a thing he could do. He wished the whole thing was over and done with. Even the prospect of seeing Happy Jack and Annie Pilgreen in a tableau together could not cheer him.

He watched to see if the schoolma'am was going to knuckle under to that brother of hers and go out into the audience to speak to the three men who were the school trustees. If she attempted to do that Weary meant to stop her somehow; just how he did not know.

But the schoolma'am was behind the curtain seeing that everyone was on hand and getting ready to begin. Johnny Satterlee brushed past him, scowling, and went out into the room to find himself a seat. By the look on his face he hadn't succeeded in getting his way, and Weary felt a little better—though why he should concern

85

himself particularly he couldn't have told.

He went backstage to get into his costume and let the schoolma'am paint his face and help him slant his eyebrows. Her hand shook a little, he noticed, and her eyes avoided his, but she kept up a chattering about the show, giving last-minute directions to this one and that one, and worrying because Ernie Beckman wasn't there yet—Ernie was to open the program with a readymade address beginning: "Kind friends, we bid you welcome on this gladsome day."

"Couldn't you cut out the welcome and just sail in anyway?" Weary suggested.

The schoolma'am told him to hold still while she fixed his mustache; but he could have sworn her mind wasn't on the job. She was worried about her brother, all right, no matter how much she might try to hide it.

A peculiar squeamish feeling came over Weary, and it seemed to center in the pit of his stomach. He turned and looked questioningly at the schoolma'am who was now busy with Happy Jack, laughing as if she really meant it. Weary shook his head. She didn't seem to feel so bad— and even if she did, what was that to him? He wasn't to blame because her brother had struck her for more money than she had to give. . . .

It just didn't seem reasonable. Maybe he had eaten something for supper that didn't set so well. He listened to the humming of voices and the shuffle of feet out beyond the curtain, and suddenly he wondered if he might possibly be scared—and the moment that suspicion was born, the qualmy feeling in the region of his diaphragm grew more pronounced. In a way it relieved him, too. It seemed to prove that he wasn't worrying himself into a lather over the schoolma'am's troubles, anyway.

He edged over to where Chip and Cal were amusing themselves by peeking at the audience from behind the tree.

"Say, how do you fellows stack up?" he whispered forlornly.

"Pretty lucky," Cal told him cheerfully. "Gee whiz, lookit 'em pile in! We oughta built a bunch of double-deck benches to hold 'em all!"

"Feel all right, Chip?" Weary pursued anxiously.

"Why, sure," Chip said with characteristic brevity. "I wonder who those silver-mounted spurs are for, right there by that gold cornucopia. See if you can read the name, Cal. They've been put on since we came, I know that."

Weary turned away dejectedly. He saw Happy Jack, who should have been paralyzed with stage fright, looking so darned satisfied with himself that Weary felt like kicking him. Even the thought of that mistletoe scene failed to cheer him. He didn't care what happened to the darned show.

Miraculously, the confusion behind the stage curtain subsided. Ernie Beckman was out there on the edge of the platform before the closed curtain rattling off "Kind friends, we bid you welcome on this gladsome day," without turning a hair. It made Weary dizzy just to think of it.

He couldn't for the life of him see how the schoolma'am managed to make everything go along so smoothly. There was something inhuman in the way this one and that one would walk out front when their names were called, and do whatever they were supposed to do without a single bobble. "Mamma!" he thought miserably when the Jarley Waxworks began taking their places in the half circle that would give everyone in the audience a full view of the proceedings, "am I the only knock-kneed son-of-a-gun in this show?"

Apparently he was. When the curtains parted and the laughter and clapping of hands had died to an expectant hush, Mrs. Jarley went into her speech with what Weary considered a perfectly sickening relish. Where before Cal had stumbled over the long words, tonight he rolled them out with a flourish.

It sent cold chills over Weary just to hear Cal go on about the terrible ferocity of Captain Kidd and the ghoulish pleasure the old pirate took in slaying his innocent victims. From the corner of his eye Weary saw the jerky, mechanical way in which Captain Kidd raised his sword and brought it down within an inch of where his Little Doctor's head had been before she rocked back away from the blow.

The Chinese Giant, Little Bo Peep (who was Pink) and Sir Walter Raleigh smoking his first pipe while a scared servant lifted a bucket of water to throw on him, were all working away until their machinery gradually ran down—and it all seemed unreal, and as if he were caught with a lot of robots (though he never had heard that word for it). And the way the crowd out front whooped and hollered brought gooseflesh all over him.

And then it was time for the Japanese Dwarf to eat his

poisoned rice. He wished Mrs. Jarley wouldn't talk so blamed fast, and he wanted to tell her that she was leaving out a lot of her speech. But all he could do was to fix a glassy stare on the audience, like a bird trapped with a den of rattlers.

He did not even hear the alarm clock buzzing behind his back when Mrs. Jarley wound him up. The lady gave him an admonitory kick and whispered, "Come alive, you chump!" and when Weary just sat there staring, she turned to the audience.

"This here Japanese Dwarf I got second-handed at a bargain sale for three forty-nine, marked down for one week only," Mrs. Jarley explained apologetically. "I got cheated like h—like I always do at bargain sales, for this Japanese Dwarf is just about wore out. Something's wrong with his inside works, and I ain't had time to take 'em out and see what's the matter. Screw loose some-where, I guess."

Cal fiddled with Weary's arms, took his head in both his hands and nearly twisted it off, shook him violently, hissing under his breath, as he wound the old clock once more, "For half a cent I'd strew your works all over the stage. Eat, darn yuh, *eat!*"

So the Japanese Dwarf ate his poisoned rice while his neighbors rocked in their seats and shrieked with mirth. There was no doubt of it, the entire audience considered Weary the star actor of the show.

The clapping and stomping of feet went on until Mrs. Jarley couldn't be heard at all. They yelled for the Wax-works to start in again at the beginning and do it all over, which was manifestly impossible; and above the uproar, cries of "Oh, you Dwarf!" were heard—so much for justice.

When the tumult had at last stilled and the stage had been cleared of the Waxworks, Rena Jackson announced that Miss Satterlee would sing "Pass Under the Rod," after which the school would sing "Silent Night," and the program would close with a tableau, "Under the Mistletoe."

"You'll have to take off your shoes and walk in your sock feet while you arrange the background for the tableau," the schoolma'am told her volunteer stagehands while she tuned her guitar. "And please don't make any noise at all. This song," she added in a confidential murmur to Weary, "is just to quiet them down and put them in a sentimental mood for the tableau. Do you think that will be all right, Mr. Davidson?"

"That'll be fine," Weary whispered back. "Kinda let them down from the sublime to the ridiculous, is the idea, I suppose."

"Those two will look funny," the schoolma'am murmured, smiling up at Weary, and went to take her place in the chair just behind the curtain—for she couldn't sing at all if the audience could watch her, she had explained.

Weary stood back out of the way of the sock-footed stagehands who were arranging a bower of pine branches hauled down from the Bear Paws. He scarcely knew they were there. It seemed to him that he had never heard such singing or such playing. The schoolma'am had never sung in public before, or even played her guitar. Her voice was a sweet, full contralto; at the end

90

of each stanza of the rather long and mournful old ballad she sang the refrain:

> "She heard a low voice,
> 'Twas the voice of her God—
> 'I love thee, I love thee,
> Pass under the Rod . . .'"

The yearning sweetness of those lines, repeated once very softly while the schoolma'am played an arpeggio accompaniment on her guitar with minor variations, stirred Weary Davidson with emotion. It brought a lump into his throat—he didn't know why. Then the song was over, and the children were lining up before the drawn curtain to sing "Silent Night," considerably off key but with a good deal of volume.

Behind the curtain, Annie Pilgreen went simpering to the place which the schoolma'am had pointed out. Happy Jack followed reluctantly, looking resigned but homelier than ever. Weary pulled himself together and undertook to pose the two for the tableau, but Happy Jack could not seem to get the hang of it.

With one ear cocked to the progress of "Silent Night," Weary labored desperately to instill at least some shade of romance into the scene. "Mamma! Don't stand there like a kink-necked horse, Happy!" he implored in a whisper. "Ain't there any joints in you at all?"

"Aw, I ain't never practiced it!" Happy Jack protested in a hoarse whisper. "I never even seen a tableau. If somebody'd show me once, so I could get the hang of it—"

"I don't know what we're supposed to do, either," Annie Pilgreen managed to articulate. "If you and the teacher would just show us—" she looked imploringly at the schoolma'am.

"We'll have to hurry," the schoolma'am whispered impatiently. "They've started on the last verse out there." She looked up at Weary. "Maybe, if we just gave them an idea . . ."

An unaccountable chill shot over Weary. For one instant he realized exactly how Happy Jack must feel. But he took the twig and lifted it as the schoolma'am moved in close, gazing shyly up at him.

"See?" he muttered with forced calm. "You want to hold it over her head, and you want to kind of bend down as if you were daring yourself to kiss her. When a girl steps under the mistletoe on Christmas Eve, a fellow has got a right—"

"Yeah," Happy Jack assented under his breath, backing off to get the effect. "Only I don't see how . . ."

Beyond the curtain the children were filing back to their places, having done their worst with "Silent Night." Lamps were being turned low in the schoolroom. Happy Jack moved another step backward.

Accidentally (perhaps) he took the curtain with him as he backed away. Also accidentally (perhaps) he dropped a lighted match into the pot of red fire, which blazed up beautifully.

Weary, looking down into the schoolma'am's eyes, froze with astonishment. He felt the schoolma'am quiver against his embracing arm, but she still smiled shyly up into his face until the audience recovered its breath and began to clap. Then Happy Jack mercifully drew the curtain.

In the red dusk of the stage, Weary felt suddenly bold. "I oughta get something outa this," he whispered giddily, bending until his lips touched her smiling red mouth. And Happy Jack chose that moment to pull the curtain for an encore.

CHAPTER ELEVEN

FOR WHAT seemed an hour Weary stood there motionless, lips pressed hard against the schoolma'am's soft, quivering mouth. He seemed suspended somewhere in space until the clicking of curtain rings sliding along wire broke the spell. He was standing there on the stage kissing the schoolma'am, and the stench of the red fire was in his nostrils, mingled with the odor of the pine branches above his head.

The first coherent thought that flashed across his benumbed brain was that he would take Happy Jack out somewhere and beat the living tar out of him. The second and saner thought was that he had better play the cards as they lay. He released the schoolma'am and turned to Happy Jack, who was clawing at a gray-blanket partition seeking escape from the stage.

"Don't go off mad, Happy," Weary said in a loud stage whisper. "We knew you and Annie couldn't cut the mustard—you're too darned scared. Sorry we had to job you, though."

"Aw, gwan!" Happy Jack retorted mechanically, slack-jawed with astonishment. "Me and Annie had the whole thing planned. We never—"

"I know, I know. But we couldn't let you turn that tableau into a farce. Some other time you can try one with Annie." His tone was so bland and so patronizing that he left Happy speechless and staring with his mouth half-open. Even the schoolma'am gazed after him with a blank look of amazement on her face.

But there was no time for argument. Already the audience had dismissed the program, tableau and all, from its collective mind, and was concentrating upon the tree. Already the children were holding their breath, listening for the jingle of sleigh bells approaching the schoolhouse.

The schoolma'am went out front and told the crowd prettily that the presents would be distributed the moment Santa Claus came to take charge. Everyone must remain in his place to avoid confusion, and Bert Rogers, Joe Meeker and Cal Emmett would assist Santa Claus.

What more was said Weary did not hear. He was getting into his big coat of unplucked beaver-skins, most of which he had trapped himself, and was casting his glance about the cloakroom floor looking for his overshoes. He wouldn't wait to put them on—he could do that outside. The thing he wanted most of anything in the world just then was to get out of there and get out quick, before anyone saw him. But he was not to be that lucky. He pulled the back door open just as Pink was coming in.

Pink grabbed him and held on. "Here! What're you busting out of the corral for? Going after more mistletoe?"

Weary kept on walking. "I saved her darned show for her, and I'm through." His high beaver collar hid his face from Pink, but he sounded very peeved. "Even took hold at the last minute and saved that tableau of Happy Jack's from being a complete fizzle. If she can't hold her job now, she won't have anybody to blame but herself."

"Well, Josephine! That ain't any reason why you should miss all the fun," Pink said dubiously. "Ain't you even going to wait and see what Santy brought yuh?"

"Nary a wait. I'd rather swallow dynamite fumes than that darned red-fire smoke. Any more entertaining done in this neck of the woods, you tell 'em, Cadwolloper, they can count me out. I don't care how many brothers the schoolma'am's educating."

They had reached the horses and Weary was untying his with quick, angry jerks. Pink stood watching him, not quite knowing what to make of this unprecedented outburst of temper.

He shrugged farther down inside his coat collar. "Looks to me like you was getting pretty good pay when that curtain opened the second time," he observed sweetly. "I don't see what kick you've got coming. The rest of us made just as big fools of ourselves as you did, and you're the only one in the bunch that's got anything out of it at all. And you're bellyachin' about it. What's the matter with you, anyway? Don't you *like* to kiss a pretty girl?"

Weary remembered his overshoes and wouldn't stop to put them on, but tied them behind the cantle instead. "When I kiss a girl," he snorted, "I like to do it because I want to, when I want to, and to the one I want to. Use

95

your head, Cadwolloper, and don't try to be funny."

As he rode off toward the rind of moon and the bright star that kept it company, he was acutely conscious of Pink's puzzled stare following him. He hoped he had been convincing, though he wasn't sure of that. It was a cinch the boys would devil the life out of him if they thought he cared, or even if they thought Happy Jack had framed him into that tableau.

But who would ever dream that Happy would think up a scheme like that? It just went to show that you couldn't bank on a thick skull never getting an idea through it. He had to admit that Happy had been pretty slick about it. Trouble was, he'd get so swell-headed you couldn't live on the same ranch with him if he thought he really had put it over.

There was another phase of the incident that troubled Weary. It was the effect that kiss had had upon him. He was girl-shy. In his own opinion he had reason to be. A girl had made a fool of him once—he certainly didn't intend to give another one the chance. And here he was, getting the blue willies over that little schoolma'am. It had to stop right there, before it could go any farther. The kiss had taught him that much. He wasn't going to go through seven kinds of hell again, for her or any girl on earth. Let her think what she pleased—the show was over as far as he was concerned.

When the Happy Family surged into the bunkhouse two hours later, the crisp coldness of the night coming in with them, with pockets bulging with nuts and candy, big red apples and popcorn balls—to say nothing of Christmas neckties, a shaving mug or two and sundry pairs of fine wool socks—Weary was either asleep or giving a splendid imitation of a man sunk in slumber. They woke him up and guyed him a little, and told him all about the tree, and gravely deposited upon his bed the modest gifts which Santy had brought him.

All this was perfectly natural and as it should be. Weary felt better. After all, what was a little plain old stage fright? What was a kiss on Christmas Eve? He drew a blanket up around his shoulders and sat up in bed to munch striped candy from the lumpy stocking made of pink mosquito netting, and fished with long fingers in amongst the candied popcorn for almonds which he shelled with his hands and ground to a fine, sweet pulp between his strong white teeth.

Someone had built up the fire and was heating water in a lard bucket for hot toddies. There was talk of invading the mess house and whipping up some eggnog, but it came to nothing, chiefly because they didn't want old Patsy to get wise to the pint flask of whisky which Slim had brought home with him—a gift from Old Man Meeker.

Somewhat to Weary's surprise, there was very little said about his part in the performance. Each one of the boys, he discovered, privately thought himself the outstanding actor of the show. Even Slim wore an air of importance over his Santa Claus impersonation. Only Happy Jack eyed Weary with suspicion. Three times he tried to explain how he and Annie Pilgreen had planned to trap Weary and the schoolma'am in that tableau, but fortunately no one paid any attention to him. They were all too busy talking at once, trying to get someone to listen to how scared they were.

It was all very reassuring to Weary. By the time he had eaten two apples, all the nuts in his pink stocking and a huge popcorn ball, finishing off with a generous toddy well-flavored with nutmeg, he burrowed into the blankets and went to sleep. Since the rest of the bunch owned to symptoms such as he had suffered, he decided that he was still heart-whole and fancy-free.

It was not until the New Year's ball, held in the Dry Lake schoolhouse, that Weary realized the fallacy of that belief. The schoolma'am was there, and it was with something of a shock that Weary discovered she was even prettier than he had remembered.

It seemed to him that her hair was shinier than any girl's had ever been. When she danced by the wall lamps and the light struck her head in a certain way, her hair had a look of polished bronze where it fluffed up away from her face. And he didn't see how he could have forgotten her eyes, they were so large and so velvety brown, and they sparkled so when she smiled.

She did look at him and smile when she first came in with the Meekers, but Weary was engaged at that moment in the grand-right-and-left of a square dance, and merely gave the schoolma'am a slight bow and a flash of his teeth as he swung at the corner.

He didn't want her to think he attached any personal significance to that kiss, so he made it a point to wait until most of the boys had danced with her before he headed in her direction. She was engaged for that dance, she told him carelessly, and went off with the bookkeeper of the store. Weary danced three more dances before he asked her again—or tried to; but she was just going out on the floor with the bookkeeper again, who was considered something of a dude because of the fine clothes he wore, and because he knew all the latest dances a little better than the cowboys did.

Weary considered that let him out. Though he hadn't danced with her, she couldn't think he had any desire to pass her up. All the same, nobody could accuse him of being stuck on her, either. He thought he had managed things pretty slick. It didn't occur to him that the schoolma'am was a pretty good manager herself.

When midnight came, and all the men had gone outside and fired guns in the air, and the blacksmith's anvil had boomed its greeting to the New Year, the four-piece orchestra from Great Falls returned to the platform wiping their mouths with the backs of their hands as they picked up their instruments.

The floor manager called out that since this was leap year now, the rest of the night belonged to the ladies. They could choose their partners for supper and till morning. There was loud clapping and laughter, and in the midst of it the schoolma'am went close to Weary, beating a Box Elder girl by the length of her arm.

"Will you be my partner, Will Davidson?" she asked in her crisp, authoritative way. "You seem to be footloose, and I rather like the way you dance."

"Why, certainly," Weary answered. But his tone lacked enthusiasm. He had been carefully building up his defenses, and now she had come along and with a dozen words or so had knocked his mental barricade flat. He saw Cal Emmett roll his eyes towards Pink, and he saw the dimples appear in Pink's cheeks. He knew what that meant, all right; and pretty as she was, he wished the schoolma'am was in Halifax right then.

Probably the schoolma'am hadn't meant anything at all by her choice, but that made no difference whatever. No scheming mother with a marriageable daughter on her hands ever set herself to more conscientious match-making than did the Happy Family. All through that dance they watched Weary like hawks hovering over a chicken yard. When the schoolma'am chose one of them for a dance, the chosen one made it a point to whisper apologies to Weary afterwards. They managed to kill whatever enjoyment he might have found in dancing with the schoolma'am. Under their keen appraising eyes he felt himself stiff and unmannerly, and it was with a sigh of relief that he swung into the Home-Sweet-Home waltz just as the sky was beginning to redden in the east.

"Your brother didn't stay long," he said, trying to make conversation that would not lead to anything in the way of future entanglements.

The schoolma'am tilted her head a little to glance up into his face. "He only came to tell me he was leaving school," she said with an attempted lightness which did not fool Weary a bit. "The crazy kid—he wants to go to the Klondike and make his everlasting fortune. Some friends of his are going, and they offered to take him along and pay half his expenses, and give him a share in whatever they find. Make him a partner, in fact." Then she laughed. "I very soon put my foot down on that scheme," she added. "I sent him back to school. So Johnny doesn't love his sister any more."

"He'll thank you someday," Weary murmured soberly. "He'll appreciate what you've done for him."

It wasn't a happy subject. They danced in complete silence after that and parted with scarcely another word. Weary got his horse from the livery stable and rode home alone, fighting the desire to do something that would make the schoolma'am's life a little easier.

CHAPTER TWELVE

AFTER THAT dance Weary knew that he would have to ride way around the schoolma'am if he valued his peace of mind. A little more and he would have made a fool of himself again over a girl. So he spent the rest of that winter dodging the schoolma'am as unobtrusively as possible.

It wasn't easy, for the Happy Family was pretty hard to fool—in fact it seemed a hopeless thing to attempt. By some occult means they always seemed to know what was in a fellow's mind, and excuses had to be good. Furthermore, the girls of the community had started the fashion of giving surprise parties every week or so on this one and that one, with no provocation whatever; and since it was leap year and the girls were using their privilege right up to the hilt, a fellow almost had to break a leg if he didn't want to go with the girl who asked him.

True, the schoolma'am didn't ask him to take her to any of the parties; not right out in so many words. But she did send him friendly messages every chance she got—or certain members of the Flying U outfit were liars by the book.

Weary didn't know when he had ever put in such a winter. Never, since the outfit moved in and located on Flying U Creek and the country began to settle up, had folks been so sociable. It seemed to him they must lie awake nights planning that giddy whirl of surprise parties, candy pulls, and just plain old visiting. The Happy Family cheerfully rode for miles in the biting winter winds to fulfill their social obligations.

But as for Weary Davidson, he took a leave of absence and went to Great Falls to have his teeth attended to. He stayed as long as he could endure the monotony of town life—which was less than two weeks—and returned to meet the schoolma'am face to face on the platform when he got off the train. All that had prevented their meeting on the train was the fact that Weary had ridden all the way down from Great Falls in the smoker, yarning with a couple of fellows he knew from Chinook.

The schoolma'am looked peaked, he thought. Her eyes were too big for her face and she didn't seem to have much color in her cheeks any more. She did not, he discovered with some surprise, seem any gladder to see him than she would have been to see Cal, or Pink, or even Happy Jack.

He took her suitcase and led the way into the warm waiting room to wait until the train had moved on out of the way, because it was standing on the beginning of the path that cut across to town and the hotel. They stood beside the big rusty stove and looked at each other.

"How come you're not teaching school, Miss Satterlee?" Weary inquired amiably.

"I got a week off to go and look after Johnny," she

102

replied, almost in her crisp direct way, not dodging around a painful subject as some would have done.

"Sick?"

"No—or I hope not. He ran away from school, Mr. Davidson. I don't know where he is, though he said he wanted to go to the Klondike—"

"Yeah, I know. You told me at the New Year's dance."

"Yes, I did, didn't I?" She looked at him with a little twisted smile. "I don't know why I should, unless you're the kind of person one does tell things to. And then you rode out from town with Johnny at Christmas, and I suppose he talked all the way, and told you all the grand things he meant to do."

"He did, all right. Plumb full of ideas—like any other kid his age."

The schoolma'am pulled off her gloves and held her fingers close to the heat. "I couldn't find whether he had actually started for the Klondike or not. I couldn't learn a thing about him except that he has been running around all fall with a pretty wild bunch." She looked up at Weary and her big brown eyes had no sparkle in them. "He stopped writing to me, is why I went to see what was wrong." She gave a sigh of exasperation. "What *would* you do with a kid like that?" she exclaimed; not as if she expected him to tell her, but more as if she had reached the end of her rope.

"Do? Let him go. Let him take the bumps. It's the only way a kid like that will ever learn anything, Miss Satterlee."

"I know—I know, that's what they all told me. The head of the school and his teachers . . . It's what I'm tempted to do. He always was a selfish brat, thinking of no one but himself. But still, the habit of responsibility—"

"Forget it. The sooner that kid learns to stand on his own two feet the better off he'll be. He'll make out. I wasn't but seventeen when I ran away from home, Miss Satterlee. It sure made a man of me in a hurry.

"It will be the making of that brother of yours, if he's got the right stuff in him—and if he hasn't, you can't put it there. Like horses—some horses never are worth their salt, no matter how much trouble you take training them. Others just naturally fall into line without much breaking." He stopped abruptly, afraid he had said too much, or too little. "It's up to Johnny himself from now on," he plunged ahead, wanting to convince her before she told him to mind his own business.

"You've done all you can for him, and the sooner you quit handing out the dough every time he holds out his hand, the better off he'll be. He's got to earn a dollar himself before he knows the worth of it."

She didn't seem angry or offended, at all. "I suppose you're right," she sighed. "I know you are. They all are. But I do think he might write to me and tell me what he's doing."

Outside, the conductor was shouting "All aboard!" The engine by the water tank began to snort and puff. A bell started ringing.

"You don't honestly expect him to write, do you? Remember, you just called him a selfish brat who thought only of himself. I'll bet," Weary said daringly, "Johnny never did write to you, hardly, except when he wanted money. The chances are," he went on hurriedly, wishing to prepare her for the young whelp's cruelty, "he won't ever write—unless maybe sometime after he's married and settled down with a family. Then his wife might get after him and jog him up about writing to his sister."

He watched the smile flickering around her mouth that he had kissed last Christmas Eve. It gave him a strange feeling of protectiveness. "When you hear from Johnny," he drawled humorously, "it'll probably be to tell you he's got a couple of boys growing up."

That seemed to strike the schoolma'am as being rather funny. She laughed with a note of relief. "I do hope you're right, Mr. Davidson. All I want is to know that he's all right and getting along. I can see now where I made a mistake in trying to keep him in school. He never was the studious kind. He always hated it. It has taken," she said bleakly, "every ounce of determination I possess to keep that boy from flunking."

Weary gave a little chuckle which was pure acting on his part. "Well, you know the old saw about leading a horse to water. You nor nobody else can cram book learning into a boy's head if he don't want it there. It's a waste of time and money. Yeah—and determination. He's taken the bit in his teeth now, and you might as well relax and let him go."

The schoolma'am settled her brown sealskin cap on her head and pulled her muff from under her arm. "Well, that's exactly what I'm going to do. If you think it isn't shirking my duty—"

Weary's laugh was genuinely amused. "Mamma! It

ain't so much shirking a duty—it ain't that at all, Miss Satterlee. It's just letting the kid off the picket rope and watching him hit for the high ranges. He's a grown man, strong and able to make his own way. Believe me, father and mother and grandfather and grandmother and all his aunts and uncles couldn't hold that kid now. And me, I've got more respect for him than if he'd stayed on at school, making a bluff at learning something he didn't want to know."

The schoolma'am tucked a lock of hair up under her cap and glanced toward the door. "Well, thank you, Mr. Davidson, for setting my mind at rest. I can see now that I should have let Johnny find a job a year ago. But I didn't, so he's taken matters into his own hands, just as you say he should do. If I have done my full duty, that's all I want to know. I'm willing to let Johnny do the rest, and make of his life whatever he can."

"That's the stuff," Weary approved. "That's the way to look at it, Miss Satterlee. You've done your part and then some. Just forget it now, and go on and live your life."

The schoolma'am looked up at him with a little of the sparkle back in her eyes. "That," she said, in her crisp, decisive way, "is exactly what I'm going to do. And I think I shall begin by looking up Joe Meeker, who should have met me here."

Weary turned and picked up her suitcase. "I'll take you over to the hotel, and hunt up Joe Meeker myself. I've got an idea I know where to find him."

The train was pulling out, small clouds of steam drifting back toward them on the wind. The snow under their feet squeaked with frost as they walked together down the platform to where the hard-beaten footpath angled across the tracks, passing close to the corner of the stockyards and drawing a straight line from there to the open space between Rusty Brown's saloon and the general store.

Joe Meeker, Weary thought carpingly, ought to have his head punched for hanging around Rusty's bar and not driving down to meet the train. But that was Joe, all over—belly up to the bar with a glass in his fist and swap scandal with Rusty as long as either one could think of a mean thing to say about a neighbor. The two biggest gossips in the country; and he supposed now when they discovered who had packed the schoolma'am's suitcase up from the depot they'd put their heads together and get up a great yarn about it.

It all went to show that it didn't pay to dodge an issue. Schoolma'am off on a trip same time he was—Mamma! All the granny gossips in the country would be on his back now. But they'd better not let him hear a word belittling to the schoolma'am, if they didn't want to tangle with a catamount . . .

They had reached the hotel porch. "Well, here we are, and thank you very much," she said, her breath whipping past him in little white cloudlets of steam. "Isn't that Joe, just driving past the stable?"

"Yeah, that's him, all right. Well—so long, and don't worry about—"

"Oh, I shan't! Not for at least ten years!" The schoolma'am's laugh sounded suddenly carefree. "That will give Johnny time to settle down with his young family around him!"

"Yeah, that's what. Give him time!"

Weary cast a hasty glance down the street and headed toward the store, hoping it would look to Joe Meeker as if he had just paused to pass the time of day with the schoolma'am. He didn't look back, but he sort of hoped she was watching him go. And he thought how good it makes a fellow feel to help someone, even if it's only with sound advice. He hoped the schoolma'am would follow it and get that worried look out of her eyes. That young whelp of a brother of hers wasn't worth it, and he'd all but told her so.

He walked warily after that, his temper braced against rumors. All wasted. Joe Meeker came down with grippe and lost his voice for three weeks; and being a regular calf over anything affecting himself, his mind was fully occupied.

And more than that, the weather turned so balmy that spring work started in March, and no one had time for parties; and about that time a train robbery was pulled off, just up on the main line beyond the Bear Paws, and rumors flew over the range like blackbirds in a cornfield. The gang that robbed the train was said to be local boys, hiding now behind their good reputations.

The game of find-the-guilty-party was played in every bunkhouse and kitchen in the country, and one man's guess was as good as another's—none of them producing any tangible results. . . .

Save one, perhaps. The train robbers remained uncaught, but so did Weary. To his deep amazement, no one seemed to know anything at all about his meeting with the schoolma'am, or about Johnny's breaking away from school. Certainly the Happy Family never mentioned either event—and Weary thanked his lucky stars for that and settled down to the silent and rather hopeless task of putting the schoolma'am completely out of his mind—or out of his dreams, at least.

CHAPTER THIRTEEN

THOUGH THE sun was well over towards the west, the heat from it was like a blast from a furnace. There was no wind, or even a breeze; and the smoke from the branding fires hugged the ground and mingled with the stench of burning hair and hide and the churned dust of the herd of cows and calves close-held.

Cal Emmett straightened up with his gloved hand pressed hard against the small of his back, and watched the calf he had just let go of scramble to its feet and go bucking awkwardly to find its mother.

"Gee whiz! Lend me a fresh back, somebody, if you want me to go on wrasslin' calves from now till midnight," he exclaimed with a grim kind of humor; and went over to the water bucket standing in the shade of a clump of sagebrush, and poured warm spring water down his parched throat.

"I betcha we ain't goin' to git through in time for no school picnic," Happy Jack predicted gloomily, and settled back with the hind leg of a calf held firmly in his grasp. "It's goin' to rain, you can gamble on that, and we got another three hundred to brand yet if we got one."

"You're bughouse," Cal retorted, putting more wood

on the branding fire. "We'll get through, all right—we've got to. Ain't that right, Chip?"

"I'd tell a man," Chip answered, lifting his iron from the two hundredth Flying U he had seared that afternoon on the twitching sides of as many protesting calves. "I'm going home, pretty soon now. I promised Dell I'd try and get home early. She's head push on the refreshment committee, and wants to make sure there's enough of everything to go around. I might have to take her in to town yet tonight."

"Yeah, but what about us?" Cal asked over his shoulder. "I'm the white-haired boy that puts picnic grub away ahead of calf-branding, if it comes to a showdown."

Chip cocked an eye up at the sun. "Well," he said with maddening calm, "there's about two hundred and fifty calves left. If you fancy cowhands can't finish up by night, it'll be your own funeral. All you've got to do is ride over and stuff yourselves tomorrow. You aren't married to the chairman of the committee."

"Well, I betcha it'll rain before we git through—it always does when we're plannin' on somethin'," Happy Jack predicted, and grabbed another calf to drag up to the fire.

Weary, wielding a second branding iron, with expert ease and precision, not far away, looked over at Chip's crew and laughed. "If it rains, Happy, we'll pack the calves into the cook-tent and make Patsy heat the irons in the stove. Don't you cry—we'll see to it you get some of Annie's cake with frosting all over it."

"Aw—you'll be bellerin' around for some of Annie's

cake yourself, I betcha! Schoolma'am can't boil water without burnin' it."

No one save Happy Jack laughed at that stale joke. They were too busy even to bait him further.

Happy tried again. "I guess maybe you ain't seen them thunderheads off there. Look at 'em rolling up! It's pourin' down right now, up in the mountains—lookit them clouds over north!" He had made the mistake of loosening a hand to point, and his voice changed abruptly into loud profanity. The calf that had been lying so still had just kicked him viciously in the middle.

Ordinarily that incident would have provoked loud chortles from all who saw it, but at the moment no one gave it any attention. They were all too busy. That little item of two hundred and fifty calves yet unbranded had sunk deeply into their consciousness, and the work was swinging into clocklike rhythm.

Word of Chip's estimate was passed by the ropers to the men holding up the herd, and insensibly the pace quickened. Now and then when he had a moment to spare, a rider would glance appraisingly at the clouds sullenly building up along the open skyline. Their movement was scarcely perceptible to the eye, yet growing bigger and blacker with every hour. The Happy Family hoped the storm would hold off until after dark, but no one dared bank on it and they drove themselves without mercy.

For a month they had known that the Meeker school would close tomorrow with a picnic held in the fine cottonwood grove beside the little spring creek in One Man Coulee. For two weeks they had hoped they could finish

111

spring roundup and be comfortably at home in time for the picnic. For the desks would be unscrewed from the schoolhouse floor and piled into the empty coal shed, and the picnic was going to wind up in a dance, in spite of the fact that Dry Lake was planning a big celebration for the Fourth of July, only two weeks off.

Days ago they had seen they couldn't make it. That rough, broken stretch of country known as the Bad Lands—but casually spoken of as the breaks—simply couldn't be rushed over. There were too many little hidden draws and gulches where the brush was thick and the grass grew lush and sweet.

The wise range cows favored such hiding places for newborn calves. It took more leg work than riding to comb these gulches for the cattle, and with a fairly mild winter behind them the calf crop was heavy that spring.

They were still camped down there with a solid week's work ahead of them, and they knew themselves lucky to have Chip for a wagon boss. Not many foremen would have turned his crew loose for a day and a night just for the sake of a picnic and dance twenty-five miles away. All they had to do was brand out those calves before dark, and they could start as early as they liked in the morning.

Such being the situation, Happy Jack's well-known pessimism was distinctly unwelcome. What the Happy Family needed just then was not facts but encouragement.

As the swift pace went on without a letup the smoke hung thicker in the sultry air, stinging more sharply the bloodshot, aching eyeballs of the boys nearest the fire.

The dust settled more smotheringly upon them, filled nostrils and lungs of the riders and roughed their tempers appreciably.

When at four o'clock old Patsy's booming Dutch voice reached them faintly from the camp a quarter of a mile away, Chip handed his branding iron to Cal and rode over to tell Patsy the boys were going to work straight through. To the tune of Patsy's grumbling, he ate his early supper, then saddled his favorite horse Silver and swung into the saddle for the long ride home.

"You can make it all right, if you get a move on," he encouraged the sweating, hurrying branding crew, drawing rein to grin down at them. "It's going to rain, all right, and it may be a Lulu when it strikes. I've got to get across Dog Creek before it's bank full—the way it's been raining in the mountains she's liable to be on the rampage tonight—but all that is just local. It'll be down again, time you get along there tomorrow."

He looked at Happy Jack, and snorted. "Pick up your jaw, Happy, before you fall over it. See you tomorrow in One Man Coulee. Come early and stay late, and bring your appetites along. Fare-you-well, my merry, merry men—and good luck!" He tightened the reins and Silver broke into the long easy lope which would eat up the miles with the least possible effort.

The Happy Family drank thirstily from the replenished water bucket, rolled a cigarette apiece and relaxed for five minutes before going back to their calves. Somehow Chip's parting words and the carefree look of him had lifted their spirits and made their holiday a near thing that was sure to come to pass—not just a pleasure they

113

had planned with no certainty of actually experiencing it.

By sundown, working without pause and with a determination no recalcitrant calf could withstand, the ropers rode through the diminished herd for the last time, peering through the dust; then headed for camp, thankfully coiling their ropes and tying them to the saddle as they rode.

Slim kicked the embers of the branding fire apart and emptied the water bucket over them with a satisfied grunt. "By golly, I ain't mournin' none because roundup's about over," he grunted. "I wouldn't put in another day like this'n fer all the picnics and dances you could shake a stick at."

"Well, Happy," Weary said with a tired grin, "looks like we won't have to drag 'em into the cook-tent after all. You'll have the chance to lick the frosting off Annie's chocolate cake all right, so cheer up."

"Aw, gwan!" Happy Jack growled, mopping his homely red face. "You heard what Chip said about Dog Creek runnin' bank full, didn't yuh? I ain't so darn shore about gittin' to that there picnic. She's goin' to break loose an' rain pitchforks an' sour apples any minute now. I betcha—"

"Oh, dry up!" Weary swung away with an exasperated laugh. "You'd find something to bellyache about if you were going to be hung. Mamma! I never did see such a calamity howler as you are."

"That's all right!" Happy Jack shouted after him. "We ain't there yet!"

But Weary merely threw out a hand in disgust, and galloped away from him.

114

CHAPTER FOURTEEN

THE BOYS had scarcely unrolled their beds and laid their weary bodies between the blankets when the storm broke over the little valley. Like the repeated discharge of many cannon the splitting crash of thunder jarred the very ground beneath their beds as the reverberations rolled back and forth among the hills.

There was little wind, and they were thankful for that; thankful too that few or no animals were in camp or near it, since horses and cattle were believed to draw lightning. Even as it was, before many minutes the air carried a distinct odor of brimstone, and even the pelting rain could not wash away the smell.

So they pulled their tarps up over their heads to shut out the lightning glare, and went to sleep praying that no great blast of wind would take a notion to come and lift the tent from over their heads, as had happened last summer.

As for the chance that the picnic would be spoiled by the storm, they were not much worried. From the look of things before dark, this storm was purely local, following the river and its more immediate neighborhood. Up around the Flying U ranch they might be getting no more than a shower.

It was during the height of the first onslaught, when the Flying U bed-tent was beginning to vibrate with the snores of sleeping men, that Weary threw back his canvas tarp with a sweep of arm and sat up in bed to listen. You wouldn't have thought any sound could have been heard above that continuous crash and roll of thunder, but he was out of his blankets and reaching for his boots before the horsemen had ridden past the tent.

"Hello, the camp!" a strange voice called hoarsely and with an indefinable note of authority, just as Weary had finished untying the tent flaps and thrust his head through.

"Hello yourself," he retorted, flapping his arms into his slicker and buttoning it as he stepped outside into the lightning-illumined downpour. "Anything wrong?" He had reason for asking that.

Behind him Pink ejaculated, "Josephine! Dead men, hunh?" as he followed Weary to the group of riders.

Within the tent others were stirring, but in Chip's absence Weary was boss, and he waited for no man now but took long steps toward the rider who had already dismounted in the shelter of the cook-tent and whom Weary sensed was the leader.

"What's happened?" he challenged as he came up.

The man on the ground swung to face him. "I'm Sheriff Colton from Billings," he announced curtly. "These other men are deputies. We've been out after three outlaws that robbed the Stockman's Bank day before yesterday. Here's two of 'em." He jerked his head toward two led horses bearing the grim burden of roped bodies doubled across the saddles.

"Mamma!" Weary gasped under his breath. Then, "We never heard a word about that. Where did you overhaul them, if it's any of my business?"

"Jumped the three of them over this side of Dog Creek

late this afternoon, just about the time it started to rain over there."

"Third one got away, hunh?"

"No," the sheriff said grimly, "my boys are crack shots. That's why I deputized them. The third one tried to make a run for it. Started across the creek just as the floodwaters came down—cloudburst back up in the hills somewhere. We drilled him and his horse both, but they went on down the creek. Body'll turn up somewhere down the river, most likely. Might be months, though; can't never tell about them things. Anyway, he'll never rob another bank, that's a cinch."

The deputies were dismounting, standing hunched against the storm, water dripping from their hatbrims. From the bed-tent the Happy Family began to emerge, forming a curious group, listening and staring as the intermittent flashes revealed the visitors.

"Well," said Weary, "I expect you'd like to put yourselves outside some hot coffee and grub. I'll rout out the cook. Let's see, four—five of you, hunh? I guess we can double up somehow and make room for you in the tent if you want to stay. How about it, Sheriff?"

Sheriff Colton grinned bleakly and looked at the others. "Well, we rode about five miles out of our way, just on the chance we could get under cover and lay out the storm," he admitted. "We had our last sleep night before last in Billings—before the robbery."

"Well, we can fix that, all right. Better unsaddle, boys, and tie up the horses to suit yourselves. I can let you have some grain for them—you won't want to turn them out, I take it. I guess I could scare up two or three sets of hobbles, all right; or you could turn the horses into the corral, if they're broke to a rope corral. Just whatever you say, Sheriff."

"We'll have to unload these bodies somewhere," the sheriff said hardly.

Weary's lip drew in between his teeth. He was not exactly chicken-hearted; nevertheless, he had avoided looking twice at those drenched forms folded face down over the horses they had ridden on so reckless a journey. "You can lay them in under the bed-wagon," he said with a forced indifference. "They'll be out of the worst of the rain."

The sheriff snorted. "Rain don't bother them birds now," he said. "Dump 'em anywhere outa the way."

Whether they really were callous toward death, or were only trying to seem so, Weary could not quite determine. Certainly the deputies unlashed those dead men and rolled them in under the wagon like so much beef. The Flying U boys stood close-grouped and said nothing. Presently, retreating to the bed-tent to continue their interrupted sleep, they disappeared, though what might be termed the inner circle—which is to say the original Happy Family—crowded into the cook-tent with the sheriff and his men to hear further particulars of the robbery.

It seemed the bandits had not made any great haul: a little over ten thousand dollars in currency, Sheriff Colton told them over his first cup of coffee. All three were strangers so far as he knew, but these two had tallied pretty closely with the description of the fellows who had robbed the train last winter. Part of the same gang, probably. The third man—the one who had been shot in Dog Creek and had gone on downstream with the flood, they believed was a young fellow seen with the train robbers.

"Looks to me like a new gang just getting themselves organized—same as a pack of wolves gangs together in the fall," the sheriff observed. "Luckiest thing in the world we wiped 'em out right now, before they had a chance to pull off any real big jobs. The darned fools, they'd ducked back under this ledge out of the rain and was dividing up the money, near as I can make out. We'd just rode up over a ridge about a quarter of a mile away and saw 'em ride in there and get off their horses. It was a cinch."

"Gee whiz!" Cal Emmett made startled comment. "You'd think, bein' on the dodge like that, they'd have posted a lookout—"

"Every fellow was looking out for himself about that time," the sheriff said with a sardonic kind of humor, and reached for the dish of canned corn which Patsy had optimistically warmed over for the men. "Looks as if they'd aimed to split up, and the money was the main object right then.

"Time we got down off the ridge and had sneaked up in fair shooting distance, they'd made their divvy and was getting back on their horses. Scattered like quail when we commenced bouncing bullets around 'em, and didn't even try to put up a fight."

"Wouldn't have done 'em any good if they had," a black-browed deputy observed around a mouthful of beans.

"No, it wouldn't. We dropped these two outa their saddles before they'd gone a hundred yards. They had over two thirds of the money on 'em, so we got it back. Feller that went down the creek had the rest on him, probably. Don't suppose the bank'll ever see that again. Even if the body shows up later on, the money was all in paper and it won't be any good."

They might have been on a deer hunt for all the human emotion they showed. They had done their duty, Weary supposed; they were paid to enforce the law and protect banks and honest business. Pretty cold-blooded about it, just the same . . .

He let out a careful breath and glanced sidelong at Pink, met that young man's eyes and turned the unexpected encounter into a signal. "We'd better go over and see about rustling beds for the sheriff and his men," he murmured and turned with his slicker stiffly crackling.

"Eat aplenty, Sheriff," he said hospitably. "When you're ready, we'll have a place for you to sleep." He went out, Pink at his heels. The worst of the thunder and lightning had passed and was buffeting the farther hills. The rain was a drumming downpour which would probably cease before morning.

"Fine prelude to a picnic," Pink muttered as they made their way to the bed-tent.

With a hand on the tent flap Weary hesitated, then turned back. "Maybe I'm a softy," he said, "but I'm human, anyway. There's some things I can't stomach. What was done with that old piece of canvas that was around here, Cadwolloper?"

"In the wagon, last I saw of it," Pink answered, and led the way.

Not another word was said. None was needed. By the long flares of sheet lightning they found the square of canvas, shook it out between them and spread it decently over the dead, weighting it down at the edges with the neckyoke and anything else they could handily lay hold of.

"Maybe they don't mind the rain beating down on them," Weary said half-defiantly, "but, by thunder, *I* do!"

"Same here," Pink agreed softly as they walked over to the bed-tent. "How'll we fix it, Weary? You sleep with me, or I sleep with you?"

"I'm straw boss here. I'll give the sheriff my bed and crawl in with you. And keep your knees out of my back, Cadwolloper, or you'll think you bedded down with a wildcat."

Then he sighed and sat down on the edge of Pink's bed to pull off his boots. "Mamma! Man hunting may be honorable—sure it is. But me, I'm willing to be just a boneheaded cowpuncher."

"Accent on the bone," Pink murmured. "Them's my sentiments, old socks. Hey, you ain't all that wide, and I know it! Move over, you giant wonder!"

Weary gave a half-hearted chuckle. "What's eating on you, Cadwolloper? Little ten-cent sample of cowboy like you can't glom the whole bed. The hem's all you need, and it's all you're going to get. Lay yourself on it and pipe down. I'd like to get me a little sleep before morning."

They were still wrangling affectionately in whispers

when the other boys came stooping in, leading the posse. Someone lit a lantern and Weary lifted his head and indicated his own comfortable bed and told the sheriff to help himself. With a grunt of thanks, Colton took possession. Weary did not wait to see that. The end of Pink's canvas tarp was already drawn up over his head, shutting out the light—but more particularly shutting out the sight of the sheriff and his men.

For a long time he lay there listening to the rain and wondering what had come over him. He had seen dead men before. Plenty of them. Back a few years, in the days when Northern Montana was really wild, and men could well take it for granted they would die with their boots on, Weary Davidson himself had fought through more than one gun battle. Certainly he had no reason to be squeamish now over a couple of dead bank robbers . . .

Nevertheless that whole bloody scene over on Dog Creek enacted itself over and over in his mind. The posse was right, of course. They'd saved the taxpayers a lot of money; you had to hand it to Colton as a real go-getter . . .

That didn't stop his imagination, though, or even slow it down. He lay there very quiet, and pictured the whole thing from start to finish; and when, finally, he did fall asleep, he was hunting in the rain for a dead outlaw swirling down Dog Creek in one of those sporadic cloudburst floods—trying to find the body before it washed out over the bar into the slow, remorseless sweep of the Missouri.

CHAPTER FIFTEEN

AT DAWN the rain had slackened to a drizzle. The sheriff and his men, intent on getting back to Billings as soon as possible, got up and dressed and had their horses saddled and their dead men loaded and ready to travel by the time Patsy whanged on a frying pan with his biggest mixing spoon.

Part of the roundup crew dressed and straggled over to the cook-tent; aliens, these; not particularly interested in the picnic but meaning to enjoy to the full their holiday privilege by riding in to Dry Lake for a few hours of relaxation. Then, if it suited them and there was not too much diversion in Dry Lake, they would take in the dance on their way back to camp.

The Happy Family heard them discussing their plans while they dressed and let them go without argument. For themselves, they welcomed the exodus, which left a quiet camp and a chance for a couple of hours' extra sleep. As a matter of fact, Weary, having finally drifted off into a dreamless slumber, did not waken at all but lay peacefully oblivious to his world while men stepped over him and around him as they made their hurried departure.

Back to back, absolutely motionless in the deep relaxation of healthy bodies at rest, Pink and Weary slept blissfully on as the other boys later crawled quietly out of their beds, went over and got their breakfast, and returned, with a lard bucket of hot water, to shave and pull clean shirts and their best pants and coats from their war-bags, where they had been tightly rolled and packed solidly in the bottom, on the off-chance that they would be needed for some special occasion—such as a school picnic and dance, for instance.

Fancy, puffed neckties built upon a foundation of cardboard and fitted with rubber band and button, to fasten over the collar, were set in place and the wrinkles smoothed out with careful fingers, the owners scrouging down to get the full resplendence of changeable silk and contrasting figures. Slim even went as far as to borrow a pair of shears from old Patsy and trim his mustache, hoping the Countess, who cooked and kept house for J. G. and the Little Doctor, would notice and approve the jaunty effect he had achieved in his appearance.

"How's that?" he demanded of Cal. "Takes off five years, don't yuh think?"

Cal looked up from shining his best boots. "Yeah, but you want to look out when you kiss 'er," he grinned. "Countess is awful ticklish, and them stubs at the corners are goin' to make her think she's bumped up against a prickly pear."

Jack Bates bent forward for a critical inspection. "Pink was faunchin' around the other day about somebody getting away with his shoebrush," he said seriously. "You want to look out, Slim. When he wakes up he's liable to think you glommed it. He'll take that mustache right off you, I'll gamble on that."

"Well now, by golly, I'd shore like to see 'im try it once," Slim rashly declared in a bellowing voice that brought Pink out of his blankets in a hurry.

"I always aim to please," Pink said sweetly, both dim-

124

ples showing. "If that ain't my shoebrush, Slim, it sure is its twin brother. How would you rather I'd take it? Hair by hair, or just peel it off like I would a coyote's scalp?"

"By golly, you ain't goin' to do neither one!"

"Think I can't?"

"No, by golly, you can't! And furthermore, there ain't no time for monkeyshines. It's seven o'clock right now, and I'm goin' to be on my way, whether you fellows ever get started or not."

"Seven o'clock!" wailed Pink, sliding his voice up to a shrill falsetto. He turned and snatched the tarp from Weary's head. "Mr. *Davidson!* Mr. *Davidson!* I've been waiting and waiting! Don't you know I *depend* on you? I *assure* you I have had the lemons all ready for *hours,* waiting for you to come and bring the *ade!*"

In the midst of the boys' laughter, Weary twisted his long body about, caught Pink unawares and flopped him over on his stomach. Then, solemnly, he delivered four resounding smacks where they would do the most good.

"I hate to do this, Cadwolloper," he said to the surprised and squirming young man. "But you'll have to stay home from the picnic, if you don't act pretty. Mocking folks behind their backs—my, my! You'll never grow to be a big man if you act like that. Now take your hanky and blow your nose, and do stop crying. Mamma! I never did see such a tryin' youngun!"

"*Trying* is right," Pink retorted, righting himself with some difficulty, since Weary had thrown one long leg across Pink's knees. "I may not be able to scatter you all over this Basin, but so help me Josephine, I'll *try!*"

"That'll be fine," Weary said amiably, delivering a

final smack as Pink rolled out of reach. "But you'd better save it, Cadwolloper, till after we get back. This is the day we celebrate—didn't you know that? Just look at that sun out there, shining on the grass. And all the little birds singing their merry lay, telling us how time is on the wing. We'd better get a move on, or they'll have that lemonade diluted down to where we'll have to chew the peelings to get any taste at all out of it."

"Don't you worry," Pink said with a vicious little twinkle in his eye. "The schoolma'am will have a great big lemon to hand you the minute you show up. Serves you darned right, too."

They were dressing briskly now, grinning across at each other. "You'd oughta been there hours ago," Pink went on, mimicking a scolding woman, "scything the wild-rose bushes away from the swings right this minute. What's the matter with you, anyway, pounding your ear till noon? Didn't your maw raise you to be a gentleman? Stalling around camp till the schoolma'am has all the hard work done—the very idea!"

"That's my system," Weary grinned. "Women respect you more if you don't wait on 'em hand and foot. Ain't that right, Happy?"

Before the glass, where he was trying to plaster down the cowlick which was the bane of his life, Happy Jack saw his face turn suddenly crimson. "Aw, gwan!" he muttered defensively. "You don't ketch me up on nothin' like that. I don't wait on nobody hand and foot."

"That's all I wanted to know," Weary cried triumphantly. "That proves my argument. You don't wait on Annie hand and foot, and you've got her eating right out of your hand."

He lowered an eyelid at Pink. "You see, Cadwolloper? If ever you should happen to get a girl—long chance, but still, you never can tell—you want to remember to follow the system. If she wants any wild-rose bushes mowed down, why, you stake her to a scythe and tell her to fly at it. Then she'll respect you. Give in, and she'll run you ragged."

Pink eyed him attentively while he stamped his feet into his Sunday boots. Weary almost had him fooled. "Well," he mused aloud, slapping his big hat on his yellow curls and heading for the outdoors, "you may be right, but I ain't so sure.

"Mowin' rose bushes is all right, and a nice ladylike pastime like sweeping off the front yard. But packing them heavy planks down off the bluff on her back, and digging holes for the picnic table legs with only a pair of embroidery shears and a spoon, kinda looks to me like labor. What if she should get a kink in her back so she couldn't dance? I bet you'd be sorry then."

"Schoolma'ams," Weary called after him with praiseworthy calm, "don't get kinks in their backs nor anywhere but in their dispositions. They might break their backs, but you can gamble they'd never bend 'em." And he followed Pink out, feeling pretty well satisfied with himself for having countered each thrust aimed at him. He was getting pretty good at it. He ought to be, he reflected; he'd had plenty of practice since Christmas.

Hurry as they might, with eating breakfast (to the tune of Patsy's complaints about their laziness), saddling their horses, shaving and dressing up in their "war togs" it was fully eight o'clock by the time they left camp, the nighthawk and cook wistfully gazing after them, and the horse wrangler waving his hat as they galloped past the grazing herd—six carefree cowpunchers headed for a good time.

With the sun already hot against their left cheeks, and the lazy breeze flipping neckerchiefs against their smiling lips, the world looked good to them and their greatest worry was whether they would be able to cross Dog Creek without swimming their horses and splashing water on their Sunday-go-to-meeting clothes.

Even Happy Jack couldn't think of anything worse than that, and broke into raucous song as he rode. The first five miles slid behind them easily, their horses tugging at the bit. That gruesome interlude of last night they avoided by tacit consent. Who wanted to talk about bank robberies and dead outlaws when they were headed for a picnic dinner and a schoolhouse dance afterwards?

As they rode down the steep trail into the rough bottomland of Dog Creek, rimmed with high ledges, they peered ahead to see whether the creek was still on the rampage, or whether the floodwaters had run off by now. As they rounded the shoulder of the last hill, they saw the creek rolling along bank-full, and their faces fell.

"Well, what'll we do? Go up or down?" Weary looked from one to the other questioningly. "We could go on down to where the Cow Island road crosses. There's a chance the bridge ain't washed out, and in that case we'll be all right. It's eight or ten miles outa the way, though, and nothing sure when we get there. Or we can ride upstream and maybe cross all of those little forks one at a time. What do you say?"

"There's the tracks of the other boys heading down the creek," Pink pointed a gloved finger. "Looks like they made it, all right. If they hadn't they'd be back by now."

"Yeah, unless they took the ferry across the river, and are doing their celebrating on the other side," Weary qualified. "Chip got across all right," he observed. "He was ahead of the flood. You recollect, the sheriff said it came boiling down the creek just in time to catch that third outlaw that tried to cross."

He couldn't quite keep all the worry out of his tone, however, and Pink gave him a quick glance of understanding. "Sure, Chip was ahead of the flood; hours ahead," he agreed quickly.

"Aw, gwan! He never left camp till after four o'clock," Happy Jack tactlessly reminded them. "Chances is, he was just ahead of the posse, and that's why they never seen him." He looked around at the others, already seeing tragedy ahead.

"Oh, dry up!" Jack Bates barked at him. "Leave it to you to think up the worst! Think Chip hasn't got any more sense than you have? He wouldn't ride into any flooded creek on a bet."

"That other feller did," Happy Jack persisted, "and lookit what happened to him."

"That other fellow was trying to beat a flock of bullets," Cal Emmett stated flatly. "I'd take a chance on any kind of crick if I had a sheriff's posse on my tail."

"That's got nothing to do with Chip," Weary declared, too loudly. "Nothing whatever. Chip wouldn't take any risk that we wouldn't take—and I'm darned sure none of us are going to ride into that creek the way it is now."

"That's right," Pink emphatically agreed with him. "We might as well go on down to the bridge, same as the rest did."

Nevertheless they swung in close to the raging little torrent, and without saying a word about it they rode along close to the bank, watching both sides. Not that they were actually worried; they were simply taking no chance of missing anything.

They had gone perhaps a mile. They had passed the ford where no sane man would attempt to cross, and had reached a willow-fringed bend where the current cut in to the bank, when Weary and Pink, riding ahead, pulled up so suddenly their horses almost went back on their haunches.

In the next breath they were off and stooping over something lying there huddled in the weeds and tall grass just out of reach of the muddy water. With a slow, reluctant movement Weary grasped one sodden shoulder and turned the figure over so that they could see the face . . .

"God!" gasped Weary, and turned white under his tan.

CHAPTER SIXTEEN

IN COMPLETE, horrified silence the Happy Family galloped up to the place. Even Happy Jack with his habitually red face looked the color of raw bacon as he threw himself off his horse and ran with the others to where Weary and Pink knelt in the wet grass, their bodies hiding all of the prone figure save a pair of legs.

"It ain't—"

"That ain't—Chip?" another voice cut in on the first.

Slim, with all the purple washed out of his face by fear, glared over his shoulder at the speaker. "Course it ain't Chip!" he growled. "You damn fool, course it ain't!"

Weary turned a sick face up to them. "It's Johnny Satterlee," he said, in a voice totally unlike his own pleasant drawl. "He's alive. Somebody help me carry him out into the sun."

"Better pack him back up there a ways, by that thicket," Pink advised shrewdly. "Somebody might come along. One of the posse, maybe, scouting around on the chance—"

"That's right," Weary assented. "Who's got the biggest saddle blanket? Get it, and we'll lay him on the blanket to carry him. He's been shot twice through the middle. It's a wonder he's lasted this long."

Jack Bates was pulling the saddle off his horse with quick, jerky movements. Presently he shook out half a gray army blanket and returned with it to the group.

"I'll fog back up there to the bushes and locate a good place for him," Cal offered, turning to his horse. "Come on, Happy, you ain't no good standing there looking green around the gills. You can help tromp down the brush."

Weary looked up, caught Pink's eye and looked away again. Both were thinking of their foolery that morning, talking about the schoolma'am mowing wild-rose bushes with a scythe, clearing a place for swings. Weary bit his lip hard.

"By golly, what he needs is a doctor, and that damn

quick!" Slim declared in his bellowing voice, though he did make an effort to subdue it somewhat.

Weary looked up from laying the blanket smooth alongside Johnny. "Too late for that," he said shortly. "The boy's dying."

When they lifted him gently to the blanket Johnny's eyes opened and stared glassily around, not seeming to realize where he was or what was taking place. He had let his beard grow for months, judging by its length. It was black and curly with the fine, fuzzy quality of youth, and it served as a fair disguise to those who did not know him well. But those eyes of his, and the dark, arched brows and thick curling lashes—there was no forgetting the upper part of his face; not by anyone who knew Ruby Satterlee. Certainly not by Weary.

With the four blanket corners knotted against slipping from their hands, the four lifted him carefully and started walking up the slope, Pink and Weary in the lead, Jack Bates and Slim following. From under Johnny's buttoned vest, when Weary turned his head and looked down at him, a fresh red stain seeped and widened.

He glanced quickly at Pink and walked a little faster. Johnny groaned and his eyes flew open again—Slim and Jack Bates saw him and told the other boys afterwards. They said Johnny looked as if he knew what he was saying, all right, only there was a terribly scared look in his eyes.

"Rue!" he cried out. "I've got to see Rue! She'll fix me up—hide me somewhere." He groaned again and was silent. Then he cried again, "I'm cold! Legs are numb—I'm freezing. If I can just get to Rue—"

132

"Steady does it, Johnny," Weary said distinctly. "We'll get you warmed up." He was thinking of the sun driving its mid-June heat into the river bottom. Then he thought of those bullet wounds and he thought maybe that numbness wasn't altogether from lying all night in the rain.

Hurrying, they reached the thicket and found that Cal and Happy Jack had made good use of their time, and their heads, too. On the other side of the clump of young brush and trees—serviceberry and chokecherry, mostly—there was an opening, a niche where only grass grew. Dragging their feet sidewise, they had scuffed down the weeds and grass on a level spot; not large, but large enough. The sun shone in there and already the grass was dry.

So that was where they laid Johnny Satterlee on Jack Bates's saddle blanket with the corners tied in knots. They stood around and looked at him, not knowing what to do next—or knowing there was nothing to be done.

But Weary squatted on his boot-heels beside the boy and laid a hand on his forehead. "That better, Johnny?" He made his voice steady, natural, and not too anxious. "How do you feel?"

Johnny did not answer immediately. He lay with his eyes closed, breathing hard, much too fast and with a harsh, uneven gasp now and then. It was the only sound in that thicket until someone moved his feet and a dead twig snapped.

That snapping sound broke the spell. "We could take his boots off and rub his feet," Cal suggested. "If he's cold . . ."

Weary looked up at him, looked down again, and began unbuttoning Johnny's vest. He pulled up the water-soaked, bloody shirt gently but with a swift precision that did not hesitate. He heard breaths sucked in at the sight of the gaping wounds where the bullets had torn their way out through soft flesh, and he looked up again with a swift glance going from face to face before he pulled the shirt down again.

"Taking his boots off won't help him any," he said laconically.

"By golly," Slim muttered in an awed tone, "if anybody'd told me a man could live this long—"

"Dry up!" Cal Emmett jabbed Slim with his elbow. "He's comin' to."

But Johnny didn't; not just then. His lips moved and he formed the word "Rue," but that was all. Weary stood up and crooked a finger at the boys and led them back a little way out of earshot.

"Now, get this," he said, with a low sternness that brooked no argument. "We've got to keep this strictly under our hats. The schoolma'am thinks he's up in the Klondike somewhere, trying to get a start. She's got to go on thinking that, see?"

"She'll never know any different from us," Cal Emmett said earnestly.

"Aw, I betcha she'll find it out somehow," Happy Jack muttered, and swallowed whatever else he meant to say when they all turned black looks upon him.

"She'll never know if you don't go shooting off your mouth, Happy. A couple of you boys had better ride on back to camp and get a pick and shovel; two shovels.

Cadwolloper, you and Jack go. If anybody asks you what you're after—"

"You leave that to us," Pink said tersely.

"Where's Pete and Tex?" they heard Johnny demand with a startling abruptness, and went back to listen. "They gypped me!" And he swore with a feeble venom. His black eyes searched Weary's face, insisting on having the truth.

"The sheriff got them," Weary told him with a steadfast calm. "What did you do it for, Johnny?"

Johnny squinted at him as if something in Weary's tone jogged his memory. "Do what for?" His eyes slid away to the other faces, then back to Weary. "I know you," he said suddenly, a terrible sanity looking from his eyes. "I rode out from town with you."

"Last Christmas. Sure you did."

"Listen. We had to have some money—get to Alaska."

"Better give it back, Johnny. Stolen money's no good."

"Like hell it ain't!" Johnny was breathing faster; his voice was more strident. "Money's money, any way you can get it."

"No, Johnny. Give it back, where it belongs. It's no good to you." Weary might have been reasoning with a stubborn child.

Johnny got his meaning. It was in Weary's tone. He drew in a long breath, and a terror was in his eyes for a moment. Then it was gone. His young, hard voice turned reckless.

"I'd have made it," he said in that jerky way, as if he could only manage short sentences with the little breath

135

he had. He was like a man who has been running from something. "They shot me—but I'd have made it—only the creek—"

"I know," Weary said gently. "You're shot bad, Johnny." His fingers dropped to one flaccid wrist, steadied there upon the galloping pulse. "Better give it back—clean the slate."

"You mean—I'm going to—*croak?*" The boy's voice shook, but he was tough. He was going to be tough to his last breath, Weary saw.

"That's what. Come clean, Johnny. Don't go out with stolen money on your conscience." That gentle voice of Weary's was implacable.

Johnny turned his head this way and that, fighting that voice. "No! Took a big chance—for that money. They gypped me, damn 'em! I'll—see 'em in hell first."

"They beat you there, Johnny. Shot off their horses, both of them. They didn't keep any money, either. The sheriff got it. Better clear your mind—"

"No!" Johnny's voice had a febrile violence. "I paid high for that money. Got gypped. Tell you what—give it to Rue. Good old Rue. If they hadn't shot me—I'd have made it—to Rue. Sis would fix it up. Hide me . . ."

His voice trailed off, and in the brief silence you could hear Weary grinding his teeth together. He didn't do that often; no oftener than a man wants to commit murder. He sat there on his heels and stared hard at Johnny's face, his underlip drawn between his teeth.

The young scamp was going fast, but he couldn't go fast enough to suit Weary. All he could think of was that the schoolma'am must never know about this. How a girl like that could have such a brother was a mystery beyond his solving.

Johnny's eyelids seemed weighted with lead, but he got them open and looked at Weary dull-eyed.

"No use—to me," he muttered like a man half-asleep. "Rue might as well—have it." His jaw moved sidewise, trying to form words that would not come; hung slack for a minute. Then he said distinctly, "Pocket . . ." And that was all.

CHAPTER SEVENTEEN

THEY KNEW he was gone, and yet they stood there for a full minute motionless, staring down at him. The silence after that labored breathing was like a blanket dropped upon them. Then Weary leaned and began methodically searching the dead boy's pockets.

The money was buttoned inside the vest: a flat package with a rubber band snapped around. There wasn't much else. Outlaw that he had become, he must have had a gun. Perhaps he had managed to get rid of it when he was fighting the flood—he must have fought the flood frantically to have dragged himself out on the bank. At any rate the gun and belt were gone. A huge clasp knife which could be very wicked in a fight was in his pants pocket, and that was all, unless a soggy blue bandanna was counted among the effects.

"Gee!" breathed Cal, his round blue eyes goggling at the money in Weary's hand. "All that dough—and he claimed he was gypped!"

"What you going to do with it, Weary?" Slim asked in

an awed tone. "Give it to the schoolma'am, like he said?"

Weary reached over, got a corner of the blanket and pulled it across Johnny's empty face. Then he stood up, the money in his hand. "That would be a swell way to keep her from finding out what happened, wouldn't it?" Even slow-witted Slim could not fail to get the biting sarcasm of the words.

He walked away and sat down on a rock in the shade of a tall clump of serviceberry bushes. While the others watched him, he counted the money twice to make sure of the amount.

"Looking at it from his angle, he was gypped, all right," he looked up to say in his friendly voice. "Eighteen hundred. They even short-changed him on the two thousand they probably told him they were giving him."

"Eighteen hundred dollars is a lot of money, just the samey. What I could do with that roll would sure be plenty." Cal Emmett heaved a great sigh.

Squatting there in the shade, smoking and waiting for Pink and Jack Bates, they let their imaginations play with the idea of having eighteen hundred dollars in cold cash to spend. It certainly was an intriguing subject, and they were still at it when the digging tools arrived. Pink had brought the square of canvas used last night as a pall and his glance went at once to the long figure on the blanket as he dismounted and began pulling at the knots in his saddlestrings.

The sight of the picks and shovels stirred something deep in Slim's phlegmatic nature. He looked from Pink to Weary and back again, and the purplish hue deepened in his face. "Say, by golly, you ain't goin' to waste no canvas nor no hard diggin' on that young skunk, I hope," he made violent protest.

"What do you suppose we made the trip to camp for?" Pink snapped.

"Well, by golly, you wouldn't of went if you'd of waited to hear what he said," Slim said heavily. "Why, the young whelp was on his way to Joe Meeker's when they got 'im. He was aimin' to make the schoolma'am hide 'im out somewheres. And he wouldn't jar loose the money he stole, not even when Weary told 'im he was dyin'!" Slim's jowls quivered with indignation.

"That right?" Pink looked at Weary, who nodded assent.

"And furthermore," Slim added vehemently, "I ain't goin' to turn a shovelful of dirt to bury 'im. You fellers can do as you please about it, but by golly, you can count me out!"

"Same here," Happy Jack declared sourly. "Put 'im back in the crick, why don'tcha, and let 'im float on down? You'll git yourselves in bad with the law if you go to work and bury him without no inquest or nothin'. Sheriff'll be lookin' for 'im in the river, and you'd better let 'im go where he'll be found."

Weary was biting his lip again and shaking his head at that. He did not say what was in his mind, however, and it was Pink who said it for him:

"Don't overlook the fact he's the schoolma'am's brother," he said, sternly for him. "Ain't you got any respect for a fine girl like her? What if he was a lowdown ornery skunk? He was just a kid, and he got off on the

139

wrong foot, throwing in with the wrong kinda friends. Sure, we'll bury him as decent as we can. I guess we can do that much for Ruby Satterlee, can't we?"

"Aw, gwan! You said yourself—or some of yuh did—she ain't s'posed to find out about 'im."

"And she wouldn't, either, if you didn't know anything about it yourself," Pink retorted bluntly. "But you never did keep anything to yourself yet, so far as I know. And the deeper the secret, the deeper you put your foot in it every time you open your mouth."

"And that's no josh," Jack Bates attested.

"Aw—" Happy Jack began furiously, but Weary stopped him with a lifted hand.

He stood up and faced them as one who has thought things through and has come to a decision. He had wrapped the money in the blue bandanna and was tying the corners around the little package in small, hard knots.

"Be that as it may," he said evenly, "we can't dump Johnny's body back in the creek as you would a dead animal's. I don't know as I'd do that to a dog, even.

"Happy and Slim, you needn't take a hand in this if you don't want to, but it strikes me we'll all sleep better if we know he's put away decently. Pink's right. After all, Johnny was just a bullheaded boy without any father or mother to hold him straight. If he had a rotten streak in his makeup, he's taken it with him—and who are we to judge?" And he added grimly, "As the sheriff said, he'll never rob another bank."

He stood balancing the package in his palm, the others watching him in silence. With a lifted eyebrow and a little, twisted smile, he turned and handed the package to Slim.

"Cadwolloper, you're an outlaw," he stated baldly. "You were making your getaway in a hurry, yesterday, and you didn't have time to put this away inside your shirt like you meant to. The posse was after you and you were hightailing it for the ford. You thought you slid this into your coat pocket, but it missed the pocket and fell on the ground. Got that?"

"I got what you said." Pink's tone was cautious and noncommittal. "But I don't get the point—is there supposed to be one?"

"Yeah, there is. The point is that I'm a darned poor liar. When I go tellin' the bank in Billings that I found this money tied up like this, I want it to be the truth. Up to a certain point, anyway."

"Well, by golly!" Slim snorted. "Play actin' a lie just so'st you kin tell the truth about it! That there beats me!"

Weary ignored that. He ignored, too, Happy Jack's prophecy that he would land in jail himself and serve him right. Even Cal, confirmed optimist that he was, couldn't see any sense in taking back that money and maybe getting in a jam over it. The bank didn't expect it to be turned in, he argued. Even the sheriff had no idea of ever getting it back.

Jack Bates, the quiet one, created a diversion by selecting a bare space in the middle of the thicket and starting to dig, after picking up a spade. It was a good place for a grave, especially one which must remain unknown if possible. Weary's heart warmed to him, though he said nothing.

Slim was not so reticent. He seemed to take that gesture of Jack's as a challenge to himself. "Well, by golly, that's all poppycock, if you ask me. Craziest business I ever seen. Me, I'm goin' on that picnic."

Weary, on his way to his horse, stopped three feet from Slim and stood there looking down at him.

"Sometimes you make me think of a hog fighting the rest away from the trough," he said dispassionately. "All you consider important is filling Slim's belly and not being bothered with other folks' troubles. Here's one-time when you're going to think of someone besides yourself for a change.

"You wait right here, and start with the rest of the boys. Show up alone, and every Tom, Dick and Harry in the crowd would be asking where the rest of the bunch was and why they weren't with you. Whether you approve of the way we're doing this or not don't make a bit of difference to me, Slim. You stick with the bunch and keep your face closed." And with that he started on.

"Well, by golly, I guess I've got a right to say—"

Weary whirled back upon him. "Say it now, then, because when we leave this place you're going to keep your lip buttoned. And I don't mean maybe!"

"Oh, go to thunder!" Slim surrendered. "Go ahead and hold your funeral for all me. Only, don't count me amongst the mourners." He turned his back and walked off, grumbling to himself.

Cal Emmett moved over and picked up a spade, looked it over, tested its cutting edge with his thumb and went into the thicket to help Jack. Happy Jack looked after him dubiously, then slowly followed. The tension was broken. Come what might, the Happy Family would stand together as a unit against the world, and their own private opinions would be confined to their own small circle.

Weary mounted Glory and rode away up the creek to find the money Pink had obligingly dropped for that purpose. Foolish, maybe; he admitted it. But something within him made it seem necessary that he should actually pick up that package from the ground as he rode down the creek.

He had to have that physical fact to steady his gaze when he faced the sheriff and the men in the bank. The sheriff, anyway, was no fool. Weary guessed sheriffs are lied to so much they can see it in a fellow's eyes. . . .

And Colton had to believe, this time. He had to draw a line through that robbery case. Mark it finished, and forget it. Only then could Weary draw a long breath.

"Well," Pink explained to Ruby Satterlee with disarming frankness, "Weary did think for a while that he might come along with us. He even went so far as to shave. I thought sure he was coming. But at the last minute he backed out. He said to give you his apologies—"

The schoolma'am gave a brittle laugh. "Apologies? Why in the world did he imagine I should want an apology?"

"Well—after going to all this trouble to get up a picnic and dance—Weary thought you might kinda take it as a snub, I guess—"

"Snub—from *him?* How funny! I gave this picnic to

please the children and their parents. I'm sure it doesn't matter in the least to me whether Mr. Davidson chooses to honor us with his presence or not. Just tell him that for me, will you, Mr. Perkins? Tell him I scarcely think his absence important enough for an apology."

Pink showed his dimples deliberately. In his experience they were what might be considered sure-fire at turning away wrath.

"That isn't the kind of message I expected to carry back to him," he said guilelessly. "He really meant that about the apology, Miss Satterlee."

The schoolma'am lifted her chin an inch, which Pink knew was a bad sign. "Then just don't tell Mr. Davidson anything at all," she said quickly. "In my opinion, there have been altogether too many messages floating around the country, the past few months."

"You mean between you and him?"

"Mr. Davidson seems to have a weakness for sending verbal messages of no consequence whatever. I find it very tiresome," the schoolma'am said primly. "And while this is not a message, Mr. Perkins, and I hope you will not deliver it as such, I feel it may be well to inform Mr. Davidson that I am not in the least degree interested in where he goes or doesn't go. And I am very tired of receiving his apologies for something I neither know nor care anything about. Is that clear, Mr. Perkins?"

"Clearer than you have any idea of," Pink said in his sweetest tone, and went off to find Chip and maneuver him away from the crowd where he could tell him what had happened on Dog Creek.

He thought he had been pretty slick on the whole. If he

144

knew the schoolma'am, it would be a cold day before she went to Weary for advice about Johnny. Pink knew all about their talk, and all he wanted was to head off any more talks of that kind. And more than that, he didn't want the schoolma'am quizzing the boys about where Weary had gone that day.

He succeeded almost too well. The schoolma'am was so determined to convince herself and everyone else that a certain young cowboy meant nothing to her that not one of the Happy Family could get more than half a dozen words with her all that afternoon. And as for dancing with the schoolma'am, the only dances she gave to the Flying U boys that night were square dances, which, as everyone knows, give no opportunity whatever for personal conversation.

So the Happy Family rode back to camp a very disgruntled group of cowboys who weren't at all sure whether they hadn't wasted their time trying to protect the schoolma'am from grief and humiliation.

Who the Sam Hill did she think she was, anyway? She was getting so darned stuck-up you couldn't touch her with a ten-foot pole, any more. If she only knew what they knew, Slim declared, she'd come down off her high horse in a hurry. Making sarcastic remarks about cowboys—she'd sure look cheap if she ever found out what a bunch of ignorant cowboys had done for her that day.

Which was only the natural attitude for them to take, since none save Pink guessed just how much Weary's absence meant to the schoolma'am, or just what had caused that haughty manner of hers. Pink knew, well enough, but he still thought he had handled a tough situation perfectly. Let them crab about her. The less they had to say to her, the safer was the secret. Or so Pink reasoned within himself.

CHAPTER EIGHTEEN

FLYING U Coulee had awakened from the somnolent condition which always held it during roundup time. Under the cottonwoods down by the creek the roundup wagons added a picturesque note to the little grove. The bed-tents, with their sidewalls looped up to let the breeze through, sat on the very bank where the creek ran swiftly over the gray-speckled rocks. For while Patsy had immediately moved his culinary domain into the mess house, where the wind could not blow flurries of dust into his cooking, and where wire screens held at bay the pestiferous flies and mosquitoes, the boys preferred to sleep outside during the hot weather. Most of them disdained even the shelter of the tent roof, and their grimy canvas bedrolls might be seen scattered here and there within the grove.

The weather, while warm, lacked the furnace heat of the Bad-Land country, and the afternoon breeze was not like a blast from an open furnace door but had instead little more than a balmy warmth which turned pleasantly cool toward evening.

Only yesterday the outfit had clattered down off the hogback, and already the long grind of roundup work seemed far behind them. Even those tragic hours on Dog Creek seemed unreal, and Johnny Satterlee was a name never mentioned among them.

Fourth of July was less than a week in the future, and what with the races and the games, to say nothing of the big dance in the schoolhouse to follow, the Happy Family was not worrying over what was past, but giving their full and undivided attention to the big event of the season.

At the moment they were gathered in the bunkhouse after supper, with the door closed to keep out the mosquitoes which were especially vicious that night, there being no wind. Sprawled at ease on the bunks they had not occupied since May, they were deep in discussion of the Dry Lake celebration and dance.

"Who are you going to take, Weary?" Cal Emmett drew a match sharply along the wall just over his head.

Weary looked up in mild surprise. "Me? Why, I was kind of figuring some on taking a long-eared son-of-a-gun called Weary Davidson. Why?"

"Well, gee whiz! Can't you pick on any better company than him?" Cal's baby-blue eyes turned big and round as they always did when he thought he had said something funny.

"Aw, gwan!" Happy Jack spoke up. "I betcha that feller Weary Davidson is goin' to pilot the school-ma'am."

"If he is," Weary returned equably, "he sure is holding out on me. I never heard a word about it."

"You will," Cal brightly prophesied. "She'll be sendin' a note over to ask yuh, soon as she knows you're back from roundup."

"What horse you going to ride?" Pink asked, wanting to change the conversation.

"Why, Cadwolloper, what's the catch? You know darned well there's only one horse I'd ride to a fancy doings like the Fourth of July. Good little Glory, of course, all shined up like a new penny.

"Not only am I going to ride him," he vouchsafed further information, "but I'm going to put him in the saddle-horse race. Bert Rogers will probably run Flopper. He's been doing a lot of bragging about that horse since he beat that broken-down racehorse last fall, and little Willie wants to ride circles around him and take him down a notch. I can do it, too, if—"

"Yeah—*if.*" This from Cal, who was spoiling for an argument. "You'd better get a written guarantee from Glory that he'll run."

"Well, by golly, it'll take more than a written guarantee to make *me* put up any money on him," Slim declared.

"I betcha if he runs at all, it'll be backwards," Happy Jack put in, "or mebbe he'll stand up and do a dance for 'em on his hind feet. You can gamble he won't run like a human; he'll do somethin' there ain't any money in."

"Oh, I don't know," drawled Weary. "I admit Glory's no angel, but he's a pretty good little horse, take him all around. And he'll run, all right. Darn him, he'll have to run or I'll sell him for coyote bait."

Jack Bates stopped snoring and rolled over on the bunk. "Betcha ten dollars, two to one, he won't run at all," he challenged sleepily.

"You're on, Jack." Weary promptly accepted the bet, though he knew only too well the risk he was taking.

"Betcha five dollars, even up, he runs backwards,"

cried Happy Jack, and laughed loudly when Weary took him up on it.

Not to be outdone by those two, the rest of the boys strained their imaginations and risked their hard-earned money betting that Glory would do everything they could think of, save run the race and win it. And Weary, who had his own pride in the horse to defend and his own stubbornness in defending it, took every bet that was offered, knowing full well that he had scarcely a fifty-fifty chance of making good.

When the talk began, he hadn't seriously intended to enter Glory in the race at all. The idea had been born on the spur of the moment because he wanted to get their minds off the schoolma'am. But once committed to the gamble, there was no backing down.

He wasn't sure that he wanted to. Glory might take a notion to behave himself and run; and, if he did, there was no reason in the world why he shouldn't win. Either way, the boys would have plenty to think and talk about, and Weary decided, before he slept that night, that even if he lost, it would be well worth the money.

Dry Lake was a public-spirited little hamlet. Every legal holiday was observed in some form or other, usually with a dance which brought ranchers and cowboys from miles around converging upon the Dry Lake schoolhouse.

Before eight o'clock the dance committee would begin walking round and round the room, shaving candles as they went. By eight-thirty the musicians would be tuning up, and the benches would begin to fill, tired-faced ranchwomen predominating at that hour.

149

By nine o'clock the dance would be in full swing, and it would continue to swing until broad daylight. For the next twenty-four hours the exhausted inhabitants would be in a coma, but they were always eager to endure another ordeal of festivity upon the slightest provocation.

The Glorious Fourth was celebrated much more elaborately than that. Various sports, such as a fat man's race, potato race, three-legged race, fat woman's race, squaw race, boys' race and girls' race, were organized on the spot and used as appetizers, one might say, for the horse racing which was the real excitement of the afternoon. The rest of the day was spent in milling around from store to saloon to hotel and back again.

On this great day, however, Dry Lake outdid itself. A matched game of baseball was organized and played between twelve-thirty and two o'clock; which furnished great excitement and filled in an hour and a half of slack time beautifully, besides keeping the male celebrants more or less sober.

After that was over, they arranged the horse races over the bar of Rusty's saloon, and the program was most satisfactory, with four races scheduled and purses ranging from five dollars to fifteen.

Bert Rogers, feeling very sure of himself and his horse Flopper, arrived in town early in the afternoon. Flopper had the record of having beaten a real racehorse the fall before, and when Bert stopped at the hitch rail in front of Rusty's place, men immediately came trotting up to inspect the horse and speculate upon the competition he would have.

The rumor had somehow reached town that Weary Davidson was going to run his sorrel horse Glory, and men wondered at his nerve. They knew Glory.

The popular belief was that Weary rode the horse as a kind of pastime to see what devilment he would invent next. They admitted that Glory was fast, all right, if he took a notion to run, but there wasn't a man in the crowd who would bet a nickel on him.

So when the Flying U boys clattered into town along about noon, they were greeted hilariously for their popularity and joshed unmercifully because of the lost cause they were supposed to be backing. Everyone with a dime in his pocket wanted to bet against Glory, and the loyalty of the Happy Family was strained almost to the breaking point, trying to keep from taking on hopeless bets without letting Dry Lake know their own private opinion of Glory.

"By golly, Weary's got to dig up every cent I lose on that darned horse," Slim muttered confidentially to Cal Emmett. "He knows doggoned well he's just makin' monkeys out of us by runnin' Glory."

Pink, standing just behind him, overheard that remark and wedged himself between the two. "Ain't thinkin' of double-crossing your own outfit, are you, Slim?" he inquired much too mildly.

"Well, by golly, it looks like another one of the outfit's goin' to double-cross us," Slim growled in reply. "All this crowd millin' around—no tellin' what Glory'd do."

With a hand on the shoulder of each, Pink bent forward to make sure no other ears heard him. "Gosh, that's

151

right," he agreed. "Glory might even take a notion to run."

The close-huddled group before the bar broke up and began moving toward the door. A self-appointed manager rolled a large square of cardboard into a crude horn and, standing outside, megaphoned to all and sundry that the horse racing would now take place. Whereupon the scattered crowd in the street and across at the hotel started hurrying toward the stockyards, beyond which lay the quarter-mile stretch of level road which was Dry Lake's racetrack.

In the vanguard rode Weary, a pleasing excitement tingling his blood. The feeling was familiar enough—he always had it when he mounted Glory for some ride that was especially important to him. It was the excitement of not knowing just how or where he was going to end up.

On the whole, however, Glory had started this day propitiously, with what Weary called his nice-horsey mood. True, he had nearly squeezed the life out of Weary when he went to saddle him in the stall, and he had afterwards snatched Cal Emmett's hat off his head, dropped it to the ground and planted a foot on it; but these were trifles which merely meant that Glory was feeling fine. As far as he could see, the crowd didn't worry him a bit; which sure was a relief.

So Weary gave every fleering friend as good as he sent, and never passed up any bet within reason. You couldn't tell from his manner that he had any doubt whatever of the outcome; but privately he sent up a little prayer, of sorts, that Glory would fool them all, including himself.

CHAPTER NINETEEN

OF ALL the good saddle horses in that country—and they were numbered by the hundreds—Bert Rogers' horse Flopper and Weary's Glory were perhaps the two known, at least by reputation, to the greatest number of people. For that reason the race was rousing more excitement than all the other sports put together.

Everyone was laughing and taking sides with Bert Rogers and looking upon Glory's running as just another of Weary's jokes—which irked him not a little.

Though the purse was not large enough to be much of an inducement, he had fully expected that others would compete against Bert's horse. There were other fast horses in the country, and Weary had taken it for granted that some of them were entered in the race. But not a man came forward to compete. Evidently they didn't think it was worth fifteen dollars to lose the race and be laughed at. It was too much like betting against a sure thing. Weary felt that racing alone against Bert made him and Glory pretty conspicuous, and he hadn't bargained for that. All he had wanted was to give the boys something to talk about that wouldn't lead to the schoolma'am.

Though he hadn't seen her anywhere around, he knew that she must be there in the crowd at the stockyards, and he hoped to heaven he wasn't going to disgrace himself before her and make her think he had just pulled off another good joke. With no other horses running against Flopper it sure looked as if he were trying to show off again.

While the two or three unimportant races were being run, Weary's misgivings increased. The crowd was plentifully sprinkled with women's hats and light dresses, and though he was careful not to look their way any more than he could help, he had an uneasy feeling that somewhere in that crowd Ruby Satterlee was eying him with disapproval for the foolish chance he was taking. She knew all about Glory—everyone did. And what she must be thinking of him right then made him feel like a fool.

Bert Rogers was the winner in advance, as far as the crowd was concerned, and that didn't help, either. Bert himself wore a smug look of sympathy whenever he glanced at Weary, though he didn't say much. They were good friends and Bert was a kindly soul with no desire to rub it in. He did thank Weary, however, for handing him fifteen dollars—because there wouldn't have been any race at all if Weary hadn't come forward. And that, Weary considered, was the crowning insult.

When they ambled away down the dusty trail to the starting point, accompanied by most of the Flying U boys and two or three from Bert's ranch, the crowd up in the grandstand (which was the top rail of the stockyard fence) hushed expectantly.

Far down the road a puff of blue smoke beside the trail was followed by the distant bark of a six-shooter. Gray dust fanned up above the road, thickened and rolled forward swiftly. The faint yelling down there grew louder as the mounted spectators galloped excitedly along the improvised racetrack.

Like a summer dust-devil the gray cloud swirled up the road, a mad drumming of hoofbeats lifting the crowd into excited yelling. Whooping encouraging words at random, the men on the stockyard fence rooted blindly until a black nose shot out from the cloud. That would be Flopper, and his backers yelled like fiends. Then a white nose and a flying silver mane showed alongside—Glory, running neck and neck with Bert's horse.

Lifting reluctantly, the dust gave vague glimpses of the black horse running with nose stretched out before him, Bert lying low along the straining neck; and, close alongside, the glimmer of red, the tossing fringe of white mane and a leaning, wiry, exultant form—Weary and that unpredictable horse Glory. Now, loud groans formed an undertone of dismay beneath the shouting.

When the whirlwind of horses and dust swept past the stockyards and on down the hill towards town, Glory led by a full length, which fully justified the groans.

Bert Rogers, with a look of deep disgust on his face, set his weight against the bit and brought Flopper down to a stiff-legged lope, then swung him around to return to the disgruntled crowd; but Glory, never slackening speed, sailed on down the trail, scattering Mrs. Jensen's chickens and jumping clean over a lumbering, protesting sow in the road.

"Come on, boys," someone on the fence yelled as he climbed down. "Weary's going to set up the drinks!" And with that, the man left the fence and legged it down the hill toward Rusty's saloon. Every man within hearing followed on the run.

But Glory did not stop at the saloon. He whipped

around the corner of the building, whirled on past the blacksmith shop and was headed for the mouth of the lane before the first thirsty individual realized his mistake. Then Chip, suddenly grasping the situation, dug his spurs deep and motioned to the Happy Family riding hard on his heels.

"It's a runaway! He's broken the bridle! Come on!" And he led the way in a free-for-all dash out of town and up the lane toward home.

They must have known at the very start that it was hopeless to try and overtake that red streak, but they galloped a mile or two for good-manners' sake. Then Chip pulled up.

"No use," he said, grinning in spite of himself. "Glory's headed for home, and we haven't got the papers to stop him. Weary's all right; he can ride as long as Glory can run. Come on back, boys. I've got a few bets to collect on that race."

"Same here," Pink dimpled. "Josephine! It's a lucky break for me, I'll tell you those. If that red devil had played off on us, I'd have been in the hole till Christmas."

Others expressed themselves in much the same manner as they hurried back to town to collect their bets before the losers managed to make themselves hard to find. Even Happy Jack was inclined to crow a little, and his face was one broad grin; which was an unprecedented mood for Happy Jack.

Glory settled down to a long, easy lope which Weary knew he could hold for miles. Now and then he tossed his head, rattling the broken bit which dangled beneath his jaws. Helpless and amused—highly elated, too, over his triumph—Weary sat there holding the useless reins and grinned as he rode.

Without a doubt Glory was headed for home. Weary figured that, barring accidents, he could catch up Blazer in the little pasture and ride back to Dry Lake by the time the dance was in full swing. For he was not minded to miss any of the fun, now that he had the town by the tail, so to speak.

As they approached the gate into the field through which the road ran to the long grade downhill into Flying U Coulee, Weary prepared himself mentally for a possible argument when he jumped off and caught Glory by the bridle. He would have to do that quietly, in a matter-of-fact way that would carry just the right note of mastery without being violent. Glory was pretty touchy about how you made passes at his head. He had to know you were within your rights and going according to the rules. Just let him see that he had the best of the deal, and the stuff was off right there. Making an unexpected grab at Glory was about as satisfactory as grabbing at the wind, and it was because he knew all this so well that Weary had sat there in the saddle and let the horse go, pretending that this was just what he wanted.

But Glory had his own ideas about being caught. With one roll of his eyes he saw that the gate was closed and tied securely with the rope used for that purpose. Therefore he did not turn in toward the gate at all, but kept along the trail that wound like a snake into the foothills. And although Weary's patience was worn pretty ragged by that time, he held fast to enough of it to let Glory have his own way for a little longer.

Where a wire gate lay flat upon the ground alongside a fence, Glory swung in at a good fast trot; crossed a pebbly creek and galloped up to the very steps of Joe Meeker's porch and stopped.

"Damn you, Glory, I could kill you for this," Weary muttered between his teeth, and slid from the saddle.

While he had the chance he moved to the horse's head, and with a dexterous flip of the reins looped them around Glory's nose with a twist that made him once more master; theoretically, at least. Weary needed to feel his mastery just then; for while at first glance the place looked deserted, it was not. On the end of the porch, well-screened with wild-cucumber vines, was hung a hammock made of cotton rope woven around barrel staves and padded with a homemade mattress cut to fit. And in the hammock lay the schoolma'am. By one lightning glance from the corner of his eye Weary knew it was the schoolma'am.

Even though she was pretty well swathed in green mosquito netting, you couldn't fool him for one minute. He couldn't see her face, and he never had seen her wear that dress before, but that high-arched number-three foot and the ankle he could have spanned with his thumb and second finger were as authentic an identification as any brand he had ever read on the range.

He had taken it for granted she was in town with the rest of the Meeker family. By all precedents she should have been there, dressed in her best and trying to have a good time. But she wasn't. She was here within ten feet. of him, sound asleep in the Meeker hammock.

CHAPTER TWENTY

WEARY DIDN'T know when he had ever felt such a shock of amazement. Panic had him cold for a minute, and yet his blood was racing. He didn't know what to do, but he thought he might be able to lead Glory down to the corral without waking the schoolma'am. She hadn't moved—she seemed to be pretty sound asleep. If he could just get away from the house, he could probably find a bridle bit. Then, by cutting across the pasture and up into the road, he could get away from there without the schoolma'am ever seeing him at all.

He didn't want her to see him; at least not where she would have a chance to talk to him confidentially. He didn't see how he was going to keep from giving himself away if she once started to talk about Johnny—and she would, that was a cinch. He had the feeling that he was about the only one in the country she felt she could talk to about the kid.

He pulled with a steady pressure, and Glory stretched his neck and nose obediently; but as to his feet, they might have taken root, so firmly were they planted. And it needed no more than that to tell Weary that this was going to be one of Glory's star exhibitions of balking.

With a sidelong glance toward the hammock, he stood there for a minute whispering things which it would be better not to repeat; and like a beautifully painted horse before a harness shop, Glory stood absolutely motionless with his eyes half-closed, at peace with his world.

The faint breeze freshened in a little gust that whirled in upon the porch, seized the hammock and set it swaying gently, scaring Weary for a minute, until he saw the girl never moved.

"Oh, darn you, Glory!" he whispered through his teeth. But Glory, accustomed as he was from a two-year-old to being darned and damned, failed to respond by so much as a flicker of an eyelash.

Weary pulled again, though he knew it was useless. Then, taking his hat from his head, he folded it together by the brim and belabored Glory viciously over the jaws with it; silently, too, save for the soft thud and slap of felt on flesh. But Glory had been belabored with harsher things than a practically new Stetson, and all he did was fold back his ears, close his eyes and assume an expression of beatific meekness.

Weary stood in complete silence and considered what next he might do. He couldn't think of anything at all that would be effective. He couldn't even coax Glory or the schoolma'am would waken; and, moreover, he knew in his heart that coaxing would be a waste of breath and energy.

He was just setting himself for another yank—a good hard one, this time—when he heard gurgles from the hammock. The schoolma'am sat up and let herself go in the nicest, most unrestrained laughter he had ever heard from her lips.

"Oh, gee!" she gasped. "Of all the fixes you've gotten yourself into since I came into this country, Mr. Davidson, this certainly is the funniest!"

"Oh, hello," said Weary with a sheepish grin. "That

160

you, Miss Satterlee? I thought you'd be in town hur-
rahing for the Fourth."

"Oh no, you didn't! If you had thought that, you
wouldn't have ridden away out here," the schoolma'am
declared, getting out of the hammock and coming to
stand at the top of the steps.

Weary fanned his hot, perspiring face with his hat.
"Well, it does look that way, all right," he admitted. "But
I sure didn't mean to wake you up."

"Oh," she returned lightly, "I wasn't asleep, really."
And she laughed again. "I just waited to see what you
were going to do about it."

Weary looked at her standing there laughing down at
him. He looked at Glory. There didn't seem much that he
could say.

The schoolma'am felt no such constraint. "One thing I
don't understand," she said, "is why you didn't come
before. Surely I haven't done anything to offend you,
have I? If I have, I'm sure I apologize for it. You were so
good about Johnny that really I'm eternally grateful. I
want you to know that, Mr. Davidson."

Weary gave her a startled look. "I only did what I
thought was right," he managed to articulate. "What
anybody'd do. You want to forget all that. You've got
your own life to live."

"Well, you certainly did take a great load off my
mind," she went on. "I haven't felt so free since Mother
died. I guess it was hard for me to realize that Johnny is
really capable of looking after himself. You know I told
you I wouldn't worry about him any more, and I
haven't."

"Worry's no use," Weary said uncomfortably. "Worry never got anybody anywhere." But he wasn't being very consistent right then. The schoolma'am had him worried plenty. Suddenly he understood that she didn't know about the bank robbery or what had happened over on Dog Creek. She was talking about the advice he had handed out last winter. He let out a careful breath.

"Well, I just wanted you to know I really did take your advice," she said, confirming his guess, "and I want to thank you for it. You helped me a lot. I've been hoping for a chance to tell you so, but when you wouldn't come to the picnic I began to wonder if I had said or done any-thing—"

"Not a thing, Miss Satterlee." Weary felt lightheaded with relief. "I've been awfully busy all spring."

"Too busy to celebrate the Fourth?"

"No-o—I went in and ran Glory against Bert Rogers' horse. Then I came right on out."

"I'd love to have seen that race," the schoolma'am observed with a shade of reproach in her voice. "At any rate I do appreciate your coming."

Weary didn't know what to say to that, so he said the thing he wanted to. "There's a good crowd in town— there's going to be one of the biggest dances Dry Lake ever had. How about going?"

"On such short notice? I'd like to, of course," the schoolma'am said, hesitating a little as she looked down at Glory. "But I never did think Lochinvar was a very practical person. I don't see how I'm going to get there." She added demurely, "Do you?"

"Well," Weary said recklessly, "I'd oughta brought a

livery rig, I guess. I never thought—everything's horse-back with me. Couldn't you ride the horse you ride to school and around?"

"Why, yes, I suppose I could—but I certainly would look a fright after I got there. You can't," she informed Weary, "ride twenty-five miles in a dance dress and have it look like anything but a dishrag afterwards."

"You couldn't wrap it in a bundle, could you—and I could carry it?" Weary suggested. "Then you could change at the hotel. Lots of girls do that. That's dead easy."

The schoolma'am looked at him, looked away down the trail towards town. She looked back at him. "You do think of the most impossible things," she observed abruptly, but with a look of surrender in her eyes. "I expect it would kill you, just about, to do things the way other people do, wouldn't it?"

"It would be kinda outa my line," Weary admitted. "Do you always want to do things just like everybody else?"

The schoolma'am laughed in a way that made Weary's pulse jump three beats. "No, I don't. I've always had to, though. And I've always envied you the ability to do out-landish things and somehow get away with them. Like coming here like this, to ask me to go to the dance with you.

"Well, I ought to stand on my dignity and remember who I am, and that when a man invites a lady out he's supposed to give her time enough to curl her hair, at least. But I don't care. If you can do what you want to, so can I. I'm going to that dance on horseback, and if the

163

school board doesn't like it, they can lump it. So there."

"Now you're talking," Weary said, and astonished them both by throwing back his head and laughing as he had not laughed for weeks.

CHAPTER TWENTY-ONE

THE SCHOOLMA'AM eyed him uncertainly. "Will you please tell me what is so very funny about that?" she asked when she could make herself heard. "What have I done? Did I help you win a bet, or something?"

Weary stopped laughing as abruptly as if water had been dashed in his face. "Win a bet? I don't get you, Miss Satterlee. How could I—"

"Can you look me in the eye, Mr. Davidson, and tell me you didn't make a bet with someone that you could come out here like this without a moment's notice, and persuade me to go to the dance with you?" She was not smiling now. Her mouth was drawn into a prim school-teacher pucker.

Weary's flush of embarrassment didn't show much under his tan, but his forehead, as fair as a girl's, turned crimson. "If you think I'd do a thing like that, you've got me all wrong. I never thought of such a thing."

"Then what is it? Is it such a joke that I should decide for once in my life that I would do something I wanted to do?"

"No-o, that wasn't it at all."

Her mouth tightened again with a new suspicion. "There's something very fishy about this whole thing, Mr. Davidson. You haven't told me the truth; not the whole truth, at least. You have been prevaricating to me. I felt it all along, but you are so plausible—when you want to be—that I failed to heed my intuition." Had Weary been a small boy of ten caught fibbing, the schoolma'am would have talked to him in exactly that same tone.

"Oh well, if that's the way you feel about it, Miss Satterlee, I guess you'll have to go ahead according to your intuition. Only, my schoolbook said that a prevarication meant a lie, and I didn't lie to you. Every word I told you was the truth—just about."

Unconsciously, and completely forgetting that he had a feud with the horse, he reached out and gathered Glory's forelock together and stood smoothing and combing the hairs straight with his fingers. "It's up to you whether you want to believe that or not," he added stiffly.

But the schoolma'am refused to accept the challenge, at least directly. She looked at him with an odd, speculative glint in her eyes, then deliberately sat down on the porch step, planted her elbows firmly upon her knees and cupped her small, determined chin in her two palms.

Just exactly what that posture signified Weary didn't know for sure, but he had an uneasy suspicion that it meant some mighty uncomfortable moments for little Willie. From the corner of his eye he watched her with all the wariness Glory could have shown in his most distrustful mood, but he didn't say a word. It was her move. He tried to distract his mind by looking at her feet, which were pretty enough to distract a man from almost any kind of trouble.

She shattered this diversion immediately. "Why don't you tell me the truth, Mr. Davidson?" she began, with a deliberate patience in her tone. "You say you went into Dry Lake and ran a race with Bert Rogers before you started out to invite me to go with you to the dance. Did you actually run that race?"

"I most certainly did run that race," he replied doggedly. "Ask anybody in Dry Lake. They oughta remember it for quite a while; or they will when I go in and collect my winnings."

"You mean to stand there and tell me that you won a race and didn't even wait to collect your winnings?"

"That's what. I came right on out here."

The schoolma'am pulled her eyebrows together. "But *why?* After being over at the Flying U for several days without troubling to come and ask me, just why was it suddenly so important—and so urgent? Couldn't you have waited half an hour, at least, until the results of the race were collected?"

"Well, no-o, I couldn't. Not very well."

"But for heaven's sake, why not?"

Weary looked at her reproachfully. "Well, the main reason was that when I began to pull Glory up, the bridle bit broke; like you see it now. About all I could do then was ride—unless, of course, I wanted to jump off and let him go to the wild bunch. I couldn't do that very well, because he'd be pretty hard to catch."

The schoolma'am considered that bit of information. She straightened and let her hands fall to her lap. "I should think," she said shrewdly, "he would have gone straight to the Flying U, then."

"He would have," Weary answered, "only the gate was shut and fastened. So he came right on over here."

"Oh! Then it wasn't because you wanted to come, but because you couldn't very well help yourself!" Her eyes were very bright as she stared at him.

"Well, not exactly. I wanted to come, but I didn't hardly expect to come right then."

"Did you intend to come out later, Mr. Davidson, and ask me if I would go to the dance with you?"

Weary drew a deep breath, looked at her, opened his mouth to speak, then closed it and looked away. It wasn't a fair question, and he had no intention of answering it. His manner made that sufficiently plain.

Then, to his own astonishment, he heard himself say, "I wanted to, bad enough—but I sure never intended to. Ever." He didn't need to tell her that was the truth, for it was written in his eyes.

A brown hen with her brood of eleven chicks came clucking around the corner of the porch. The school-ma'am stared fixedly at them, though it is doubtful whether she saw them at all.

"Am I such a dangerous person, then?" she asked, keeping her gaze upon the hen.

"Maybe not to some." Weary didn't look at her at all. He was very busy making every hair in Glory's forelock lie straight and even.

The silence between them had a tingling, electric feeling. It lasted while the hen found a brown-and-yellow-striped caterpillar and called her chicks about her, explaining that this was food, and they mustn't mind because it was fuzzy.

The schoolma'am watched the little domestic drama intently. Weary was just as intent upon giving Glory a straight flat bang which the first toss of his head would set flying. The schoolma'am jumped up so suddenly that Weary was almost as startled as were the hen and chickens.

"Well," she said brightly, "this isn't getting ready, is it? Since you are here, and since you did invite me to the dance and I did accept the invitation, I may as well go. That is, unless you think I'm too—dangerous."

"I'll take a chance, now I'm started," Weary retorted, his tone laconic.

CHAPTER TWENTY-TWO

"WELL, WHY don't you take Glory down to the stable and pull off the saddle for a while?" the schoolma'am asked unexpectedly. "I'll fix some lemonade and we'll eat something first. I hope your ride gave you an appetite, because I haven't had my lunch yet, and Mrs. Meeker left me two cakes and two kinds of pie, and a whole roasted chicken. And she had marvelous luck with her bread yesterday. Don't you really need refreshment, after all you've been through, Mr. Davidson?"

It would have amazed the Happy Family to see how quickly Weary came to life. "Mamma! That sure listens good," he said fervently. "You're on—I mean, it sure sounds tempting."

"I like your first acceptance better," the schoolma'am said in her quick way that stopped just short of being snappy. Her classroom tone, no doubt; pleasant enough, but with that note of authority which does not encourage contradiction. "How would you like some fresh radishes and lettuce? I can pull them and have them ready in no time."

"Sounds good to me."

"All right, then. Give me ten minutes, but don't be any longer. We haven't too much time. I don't," said the schoolma'am, "intend to travel as fast to town as you did coming out here, Mr. Davidson."

Weary grinned. "Don't worry, you couldn't to save your life. Not on that nag Joe gave you to ride."

"At least he'll go when I tell him to," the schoolma'am gibed. "Apparently your wonderful Glory horse won't. Is he balky? I never heard of that being one of his accomplishments."

"He was when he got here. I couldn't say what he is now. Just what is least expected of him, you can gamble on that."

With that open mind, he laid hand upon the bridle-rein still looped with a half-hitch over Glory's nose, and, just to show how unexpected he could be, at the first touch Glory moved off with a docility nothing short of miraculous. With a preoccupation quite remarkable, Weary led him down to the stable, without a thought of anything unusual in Glory's behavior.

When he had finished the ritual of caring for the horse, he went over and sat down on the oats box and smoked two cigarettes while he pondered. . . .

You couldn't fool her. Just when you thought you'd put it over, she'd take up the slack and there you were, front-footed before you ever knew there was a noose spread for your feet. Mamma! Put her on a good cutting horse with a rope in her hand, and she'd have the herd all worked while you were shaking out your loop. She would if she could handle a grass rope like she could words.

So now she knew he hadn't come here just to take her to the dance. Over his second cigarette he decided that was maybe a good thing. Of course, she had wormed it out of him that he thought she was dangerous to his peace of mind, but Weary thought he saw how he could fix that all right. She had him down for a josher, anyway. Let her make up her mind that he was joshing about that. When it came to that, let him make up his own mind that he hadn't meant it. He had long ago learned to be wary of a girl who tricked you into saying things you hadn't meant to, and that wariness returned now in full force.

A gleam came into his eyes which had not been there before. He stood up and thoughtfully surveyed himself, brushed bright sorrel hairs from his coatsleeve, stooped and tried to pinch creases into the knees of his trousers; took off his hat and polished it with the sleeve he had just brushed so carefully, pinched four big dimples into the crown, turned it around three times for critical inspection and placed it upon his head at a studiously unstudied angle. He took off his white-silk neckerchief, shook it out and inspected it critically for sweat stains; and found them. So he folded the square cunningly to hide the marks, folded it again and again until the corners were just the size he liked best, and retied it around his neck in a tricky knot he had learned from a sailor.

He was ready to go. He slapped Glory affectionately

upon a sorrel rump as he passed, and came near getting kicked into eternity for his pains. So feeling once more master of the situation, he swung off up the path whistling "In the Good Old Summertime" under his breath.

The brown hen, having yielded to the tired cheepings of her family, was hovering her chicks in the shade of a bush close by the trail; and when Weary came striding along in his high-heeled boots, she brustled her feathers and cried "*Kr-kr-kr!*" in a tone that sent her chickens burrowing deeper under the feathers. But Weary neither saw her nor heard her. He was conscious only of the thrill of showing the schoolma'am that he could look danger—even her brand of danger—in the face and never bat an eye.

The schoolma'am had changed her light dress for a riding skirt and white shirtwaist, and had fluffed her hair into a soft pompadour and rolled it smoothly on top of her head. Weary wished she would always do her hair that way, but he had no intention whatever of telling her so, nor of giving her any hint that he had noticed the change.

She could make splendid lemonade, too, he discovered. He permitted his appreciation there to be physically apparent. He praised Mother Meeker's pies and her cake and her roast chicken and bread, and ate three fat red radishes one after the other, biting them neatly in the middle with his teeth which he didn't know were so white and handsome they held the schoolma'am's gaze entranced whenever he smiled.

He had set himself to be casual with her; to be every

inch the cowboy who has no thought for anything save his own little affairs. So presently he was describing the race to her and making her laugh over the taunts and gibes that would have to be swallowed by the men who had made them.

Before he knew it, the schoolma'am was helping him reckon his winnings, which were quite complicated since he had been offered all sorts of odds and had accepted them jauntily without counting the possible loss.

The schoolma'am told him his recklessness was appalling, and she should think Fate would have taken the opportunity to teach him a lesson he would never forget.

"I guess that's about right," Weary meekly admitted. "Still, I've noticed Fate is a square shooter, give him half a chance."

The schoolma'am looked up from her figuring. "The Fates," she informed him in her schoolteacher tone, "were supposed to have been three old women, Mr. Davidson, winding in the thread of men's lives."

"That sure does account for a lot," Weary observed cryptically. "It must be when they get bogged down in an argument that a fellow manages to slip in a little good luck under their noses."

The schoolma'am eyed him severely. "Your opinion of women, Mr. Davidson," she informed him, "seems quite as illogical as your methods of gambling." She bit her lip. "I can't for the life of me see how anyone as reckless as you are manages to come out of your escapades so easily."

"I should have died young. Drowned myself in a well, or something."

The schoolma'am refused to answer that, but set down more figures with precise little jabs of her pencil. Watching her dark head bent over the paper and wondering what thoughts were going round inside it, Weary almost forgot that he had set himself to teach her a little lesson. He was playing with fire and he knew it, but in that mood he didn't care.

"Well," she looked up to say finally, "it certainly does seem a shame that you should take such awful chances and win all this money. Nearly two hundred dollars, and a lot of it is from your own outfit. I should think you'd be ashamed!"

Weary looked at her and knew she didn't mean a word of that. Her eyes were too full of sparkle, and her mouth twitched a little at the corners, wanting to laugh. He stood up and grinned down at her.

"Mamma! All that money waiting for me in town, and we set here not doing a darned thing about it! I'll go get the horses ready. It's time we hit the trail."

And with that he swept his hat up off the floor, clapped it on his head at a most impudent angle and was gone, taking the porch in one stride and a jump that ignored little conveniences such as steps.

He was gone less than ten minutes, but the schoolma'am was waiting on the porch when he led Glory and the little gray she always rode up to the house. She came down the steps with a large, white pasteboard box in her arms.

"You get on your horse," she commanded, "and I'll

hand you the box. I can mount alone very nicely—in fact I prefer it. I hope that box isn't going to be too awkward for you to carry, but a bundle would ruin my organdy. It's all ruffles and tucks, and I spent two whole hours yesterday at the ironing board, getting it pressed for this dance. So do be careful, won't you?"

With his back to her and his toe in the stirrup, Weary flung assurance over his shoulder. Bewilderment held him. She got her dance dress ready yesterday, hunh? She'd planned on going, all right, and he didn't need to be told who she had hoped would take her there.

It was disconcerting, that unintended revelation of her hopes and her expectancy. Or maybe it wasn't unintended, either. Maybe she just said that to devil him. Women were deep. She knew darned well how close she had come to being left in the lurch. No man on earth—nor a woman either—could have guessed that Glory would break his bit and run away to Meeker's.

By the time he was settled in the saddle and reaching down for the box, he was thinking with a faint resentment that the schoolma'am had just said that to get a rise out of him, and it wasn't going to work. She wasn't going to make a fool of him; not if he knew it. And then a sudden inspiration set him grinning down into her face. Glory had got him into this jackpot, now let Glory get him out again.

It was just a fleeting thought, at most a hope he scarcely expected to see fulfilled; and yet, knowing Glory as he did, he might have known just about what would happen.

Glory rolled his eyes at the big white box in Weary's

arms, but he didn't do anything about it until the schoolma'am was settled in the saddle and had gathered her reins up in her left hand as she had been taught to do.

Then, without further delay, he dropped his nose down between his knees, humped his back and leaped straight into the air, coming down with a pile-driver force calculated to snap Weary's head from his shoulders. From there on he wove a pattern of his own devising through the sage, heading in the general direction of the gate into the main road.

Behind him the schoolma'am was spurring the little gray and calling frantically, "Stop him, why don't you? Or give me that box!"

Weary would have liked to do so, but already Glory was halfway to the gate and there was nothing to do but ride.

The little gray was no racehorse, but his wind was good, and with urging he kept the red streak in sight during most of that ride to town. For the rest of the time the schoolma'am rode by faith.

At the mouth of the lane, however, she found her escort waiting for her, the white box still in his arms. "Do you always escort a lady to a dance like this?" she inquired too sweetly.

"Blame it on the three old women," Weary answered blandly. "They must have framed that up with Glory themselves."

The schoolma'am looked at him, bit her lip, and looked away. And though the small remainder of the trip was decorous, and the dance was all one could ask of a Fourth of July dance in Dry Lake, the schoolma'am carried two deep lines between her fine dark eyebrows, and whenever she looked at Weary he saw a question or two in her eyes.

All of which pleased him beyond all reason, and made him feel very sure of himself; which should have warned him to beware—though it did not.

CHAPTER TWENTY-THREE

WEARY RODE stealthily around the corner of the little frame schoolhouse and was not disappointed. The schoolma'am was sitting unconventionally upon the doorstep, her back turned to him and her face turned to the trail by which a man would naturally be supposed to approach the place. Her hair was shining darkly in the sun, and the shorter locks were blowing about her face in a downright tantalizing fashion which made a man want to brush them back and kiss the spot they were caressing so wantonly.

She was humming a tune softly to herself. Weary caught the words, sung absently, under her breath:

"Didn't make no blunder, you couldn't confuse him,
A perfect wonder, you had to choose him!"

"Whistling Rufus" was highly favored among the cowboys but it sounded strange coming from the school-ma'am, who had never seemed in the least inclined toward anything so undignified.

The wind, blowing toward him, had prevented her hearing his approach. She seemed to be very busy about something, and Weary, craning his neck in a vain attempt to see over her shoulder, wondered what in the world she was up to. Also, he wished he knew what she was thinking about. From the way she kept looking toward the trail by which he usually arrived, he felt justified in hoping she was thinking of him.

At that moment Glory showed the unmistakable intention of sneezing; and Weary, catching a glimpse of the object in Miss Satterlee's hand, hastened to make his presence known.

"I hope you aren't limbering that weapon of destruction up on my account, Schoolma'am," he observed mildly.

The schoolma'am jumped and turned a startled glance over her shoulder as she slid something out of sight under her ruffled white apron.

"Will Davidson, how long have you been standing there? I believe you'd come straight down from the sky or straight up from the ground if you could possibly manage it. Why can't you come along the trail, and not jump out at people like a—a banshee?"

"Mamma! Not a time do I see you, Schoolma'am, that I don't learn something. Here I've been going along through life thinking all the time that banshees stayed off in the dark and howled fatal warnings at folks! I never knew they jumped out at you."

Weary swung a long leg over Glory's rump and came lightly to earth, immediately taking possession of the vacant half of the doorstep. The schoolma'am obligingly drew her skirts aside to make room for him—an inconsistent movement not well in keeping with her

177

eyebrows which were conspicuously disapproving.

"Let's have a look at that cannon you're hiding under your apron," he said, disregarding her frowning stare. "Now, where in the world did you resurrect that relic?" He held it up and was looking it over critically. "Outa some Indian grave, I'll bet."

"I did not!" The schoolma'am was still trying to be indignant at the trick he had played. "I'm no grave robber."

Weary, still examining the weapon with interest, let the denial pass. "It won't go off sudden and unexpected, will it? What kind of shells—oh mamma!" He pushed his hat back off his forehead with a boyish gesture, held the gun the length of his arm away and regarded it gravely.

It was an old "bulldog" revolver, so freckled with rust that it bore a strong resemblance to certain noses which Miss Satterlee looked down on daily from her little platform. The cylinder was plugged with rolls of drab cotton cloth, in a crude imitation of real bullets. Obviously it was during the plugging process that the schoolma'am had been interrupted, for a gray string hung limply from one cylinder. As a whole, the ancient weapon did not look particularly formidable, and Weary's lips twitched.

The schoolma'am's cheeks were pink with confusion. "A tramp came by here the other day, and—I was just a little bit frightened, he looked so rough," she explained. "So Mrs. Meeker found this up in the loft, and she thought it might do to—bluff folks with."

Weary aimed carefully at a venturesome and highly inquisitive gopher, and with some effort pulled the rusty trigger. The gopher stood up on his hind feet and chittered derisively at the sound.

"There. You see? It even insults that gopher. You couldn't scare a blind man with that heirloom—say! If you go pouting up your lips like that again, something's liable to happen to them. You oughta know there's a limit to what a man can stand."

The schoolma'am hastily drew her mouth into a prim, untempting red streak, for she had not seen Weary Davidson twice a week on an average for the last three months, nearly, without learning that he was not a young man who could be bluffed.

"Of course," she said indignantly, "you can make fun of it, but all the same it's better than nothing. It answers the purpose, anyway. Just having a gun in your hand is some protection."

Weary turned and looked down at her—something he had acquired a great fondness for doing. "Protection from what? Unless you learn to throw straight, and figure on laying a man out cold with it—if you want a gun, why get one that can back up your bluff. You can have mine, if you'll let me teach you how to shoot with it, and satisfy myself you won't go blowing yourself to pieces with it."

"No, thank you," the schoolma'am declined in what Weary called her uppish tone. "I really think this one will serve the purpose just as well."

"That's just because you don't know the difference." Weary reached backwards and pulled his own very competent and well-kept gun from its holster. "Now here," he said, "is a real gun. We'll say that gopher over there is a tramp. All right, you saw how insulting he was over

179

that thing you call a gun; now here's the difference."

With a supple movement of the wrist he raised the gun, brought it down again and fired with a negligent precision. The effect certainly was different. The gopher leaped and rolled backwards and then lay still. Miss Satterlee gave a shrill, startled scream and jumped up from the doorstep, palms pressed hard against her face.

"See the difference, Schoolma'am? If you carry a gun, you always want to have one that's ready and willing to do business on short notice." Weary raised innocent eyes to her face, then proceeded to polish the gun carefully with a handkerchief.

"You try it," he urged. "I'll let you keep it if you can prove to me that it's safe with you. I'd hate to have you shooting yourself accidental."

The schoolma'am did not take the gun he was holding out to her butt-first. She had frequently boasted that she never screamed, no matter how scared she was. She had said that she hated screaming women, so now she was very angry. She put her hands behind her and stood there accusingly, looking at Weary with the expression which never failed to make sundry small Beckmans and Pilgreens squirm on their benches.

"Mr. Davidson [not Weary Davidson, nor even Will Davidson, as she had formed the habit of calling him] you have killed my pet gopher. All summer I have fed him, and he would eat out of my hand. Such wanton cruelty is absolutely beyond the pale."

"What pail?" Weary's eyes were still innocent.

"The pale of decency," said the schoolma'am, biting off the words. "Decency and self-respect. I am astounded at such an exhibition on the part of someone whom I had come to consider a gentleman."

"That," said Weary mildly, "was the gentlemanly thing to do, Schoolma'am. A lot more polite than to argue with a lady. That was done in the interests of science, to demonstrate the difference between a real gun and a rusty old hunk of iron that wouldn't fool a two-year-old kid." He added placatingly, "Don't be mad, Schoolma'am. I'll get you another gopher."

"That," the schoolma'am retorted in her most frigid tone, "has nothing to do with it. You could have shot at a rock or something, if science demanded that you should shoot without giving a person any warning.

"I simply cannot understand the depraved instinct that would prompt a man to brutally destroy a life which in no way menaces his own—or even interferes with his comfort. You may apologize to me; you may even be sincerely repentant—" her tone implied considerable doubt of that—"but you are powerless to return the life you have so heedlessly taken. You have revealed a low, brutal trait—"

Just then a tiny, dry-weather whirlwind swept around the corner, caught ruffled white apron and blue skirt in its gyrations and, pushing them ruthlessly to one side and lifting them a little, gave Weary a brief, distracting glimpse of two small slippered feet and the slim ankles above them. The schoolma'am blushed and retreated to the doorstep, but she did not sit down. She stood straight and displeased before him, hands pressed against her thighs to prevent a repetition of the embarrassing incident.

Weary tipped his head to one side so that he might look up at her from under his hatbrim. "I'll get you six gophers," he offered soothingly. "The woods are full of them."

The angry brown eyes of the schoolma'am swept the barren hills contemptuously. She would not even look at him. "Pray do not inconvenience yourself, Mr. Davidson. It was not the gopher I cared so much about, it was the principle."

Weary sighed and slid the gun back into its holster. It seemed to him that the schoolma'am was pretty unreasonable at times. "All right, I'll get you another principle, then."

"Mr. Davidson," she said sharply, "you are being perfectly odious!"

"Is that something nice?" Weary gave her a trustful smile.

"Odious," the schoolma'am explained haughtily, "is not something nice. Odious, Mr. Davidson, is a synonym for hateful, obnoxious, repulsive, disagreeable, despicable—"

"I never did like cinnamon anyhow," put in Weary cheerfully.

"I did not mention cinnamon—I said—"

"Say, I wish you'd wear your hair like that all the time," he observed irrelevantly, looking up at her with his sunniest smile.

The schoolma'am stamped her foot. "Oh!" she cried fiercely. "For heaven's sake don't try to change the subject! You simply make me weary."

"*Mrs.* Weary," he corrected her complacently. "That's

the mark I've been aiming at."

"You aim wide of the mark, then," she retorted icily, though confusion waved a red flag in either cheek.

"Oh, I don't know," he drawled. "A minute ago you were roasting me because my aim was too good." He pointed that remark with a glance toward the gopher which was stretched upon its little striped back, its four small feet turned pitifully up to the sunny blue sky.

"If you had one atom of decency, you'd be ashamed to mention that tribute to your diabolical marksmanship!"

"Oh, mamma!" Weary ejaculated under his breath, and fumbled in a pocket for the makings. "*I* never mentioned all those things, it's you that keeps on mentioning them. I wish you wouldn't. I like to hear you talk, all right, and throw those big words as easy as heeling a calf. But I wish you'd let me choose your subject for you."

"Oh, you *do!*" The schoolma'am's tone was bitterly sarcastic.

"I sure do. I could give you a subject where you could use words just as high, wide and handsome, and a heap more pleasant. Words like *admiration* and *felicitation* and *exhilarating, ecstatic osculation . . .*" He stopped to run the edge of a cigarette paper along his tongue.

It was just as well he did stop there. There was no need of making the schoolma'am any madder.

"If you came here today to make me hate you," she gritted, "you have accomplished your purpose admirably! It would be advisable now for you to beat it!"

That incongruous last expression struck Weary as very funny. He threw back his head and laughed and laughed, while the match he had just lighted flared, sent up a blue thread of brimstone smoke, licked along the white wood and seared his fingers painfully before he dropped it.

The schoolma'am turned abruptly and went inside, put on her hat and got the small tin lard bucket which had held her lunch. She came out and slammed the door, turned the key with a spiteful emphasis and was pulling on her buckskin gauntlets before Weary could stop laughing.

"Before I go," she said crisply, "I wish to inform you that I consider you not only odious, but all the synonyms I mentioned. And you needn't expect to escort me to the Labor Day dance, either. I shall go with Joe Meeker."

And with that she stepped past him and started off down the short-cut path to Meeker's.

CHAPTER TWENTY-FOUR

WEARY GAVE her a startled glance. This seemed to him to be carrying her fit of temper rather far, but of course she didn't really mean it; the schoolma'am, as he had learned in the past three months, was an awful little bluffer.

"Don't go off mad," he called after her. "I'm sorry I killed your gopher—on the square I am. I just didn't think; that's a bad habit I've got, not thinking. Say, what's the matter with that gray horse? Don't you ride him any more?"

The schoolma'am had taken a few steps and stopped, evidently in some difficulty with her glove. From the look of her, no human being was within a mile, yet she did deign to answer Weary's last question.

"I enjoy walking," she said distantly, as if she were speaking to a stranger.

Weary thought of something else. "Say! Come on back, Schoolma'am, and we'll have a funeral. It isn't every common scrub gopher that can have a real funeral with mourners and music when he goes over the Big Divide. He oughta appreciate the honor. I know I would, if it was me."

The schoolma'am had her glove on now, and was continuing to walk slowly down the path. Apparently she had not heard a word of what Weary was saying.

He tried again. "Say! I'll sing a song over him, if you'll wait a minute. I know two whole verses of 'Bill Bailey,' and the chorus of 'Good Old Summertime.' I can shuffle the two together and have quite a song, don't you think?"

There was no answer, nor any sign.

"Say! you never heard me sing, did you? It's worth waiting for—only you want to hang tight to something when I start in. Come on, Schoolma'am, I'll let you be the mourner."

The words reminded him of something he had been studiously schooling himself to forget. He swallowed the thought and continued to wheedle. If he let her get away now with that mad on, it would take him a full week to make up with her again.

"Say, *Tee-e*-cher!"

The schoolma'am refused to stop or turn her head a fraction of an inch. She had a quick temper, and it took a pretty good-natured young man to get along with her. Weary secretly prided himself on being able to handle her moods. She was a good deal like Glory. It didn't do to take either one too seriously, or they put you on the run every time. You had to kid them out of their tantrums.

But for the first time that plaintive "*Tee-e*-cher" failed to bring any response. He looked after her dubiously. Her shoulders were thrown well back and her feet set their small prints firmly in the yellow dust of the trail. In a minute she would be quite out of sight down in the hollow. Weary got up, took two long steps and picked up Glory's trailing bridle-reins. He swung into the saddle and rode after her.

"Say! You wouldn't get mad over a little thing like that, would you?" he asked when he had overtaken her. "You know I didn't mean anything at all."

"I do not consider it a little thing," the schoolma'am said icily, "and whether you meant it or not, you certainly did it."

"Well, how many times must I say I'm sorry? Say, you don't look so pretty when you're mad. You've got dimples, remember; deeper than Cadwolloper's, even. God only gives dimples to people that're willing to show them once in a while."

He swung off Glory and walked just behind her in the trail, leading the horse. "Honest, I wouldn't have hurt your feelings for the world. Come on and sit down on this rock, and let's talk this thing over."

The schoolma'am walked straight past the rock without looking toward it. Weary followed in silence for another two rods.

"Don't you want to ride Glory a ways? He's real good today. He put in the whole of yesterday working out all

186

the cussedness that's been accumulating in his system for a week, so he's dead gentle. Come on and try him, Schoolma'am. You'll be the first woman that ever sat in my saddle or rode a horse outa my string. Come on and see how nice he is."

"No, thank you," said the schoolma'am. "I much prefer to walk."

Weary sighed deeply, but he clung to his patience and his good nature as was his habit. It took a great deal to rouse the stubbornness in him. Perhaps the schoolma'am was trying to find out just how much it took.

"Say, you'd have died laughing if you'd seen old Glory yesterday, Schoolma'am. He like to have scared Slim plumb to death. We were working in the big corral and Slim got down on one knee to fix his spur. Glory saw him kneel down, and gave a running jump and went clear over Slim's head. Slim hit for the closest fence, and never looked back till he was over it and on the other side. Mamma! You should have heard the boys devil Slim afterwards!"

The schoolma'am gave no sign that she heard, and it began slowly to dawn upon Weary that she did not intend to thaw that evening. He was walking alongside her now where the trail had widened, and he glanced at her sidelong with a certain look in his eyes which had not been there five minutes before.

Presently he turned without a word and mounted Glory. Still without speaking, he wheeled the horse and loped back along the trail to the road, leaving the school-ma'am to think what she pleased.

The next morning she went very early to the school—

for what reason she did not explain to anyone. A meadowlark on the doorstep greeted her with a short, sweet ripple of sound, then flew to a near-by sagebush and watched her curiously. She looked about her half-expectantly, then walked straight across the bare yard to a point at the fringe of bushes.

A small, fresh mound of earth marked the spot where the dead gopher had lain, and a narrow strip of shingle stood upright at the end of the grave. Upon the shingle was scratched with a knife in large, fairly symmetrical letters:

GONE BUT NOT FORGOT

Had the shingle been wider that last word would probably have been given its full quota of syllables. As it was, the last three letters were rather cramped. There were marks of high-heeled boots in the loose soil about the grave, and that was all.

The schoolma'am did a most unusual thing. She glanced around to make sure no one was in sight, then knelt and patted the small mound smooth with her palms. Then, quickly, she pressed her lips upon the brief epitaph. When she stood up her cheeks were scarlet and her mouth was half-smiling and tender.

Weary was not there to see her. He was twenty miles away busily engaged in chastising Glory; and, being fully preoccupied, he was not attuned to any telepathic messages, then nor during the rest of the day; nor even that night, when the schoolma'am lingered very late at the schoolhouse doing nothing but watch the trail where it lay brown and utterly deserted on the top of the hill a quarter of a mile away.

She had a profusion of papers scattered over her desk, and had Weary appeared in the doorway she would undoubtedly have been discovered hard at work and very much astonished at seeing him. It is probable, too, that Weary would have found her quite as unapproachable as she had been that last evening, entrenching herself behind a wall of dignity and correct English.

When the shadow of the schoolhouse crept somberly away to the very edge of the gully, the schoolma'am gathered up the papers on the desk, bundled them inside the drawer and turned the key with a snap, jabbed three hatpins viciously into her hat and her hair and went home, walking very fast along the trail.

The next night papers strewed the desk as before. But the schoolma'am stood by the window, her elbows planted on the unpainted sill, frankly watching the trail. Her eyes were big and wistful, and her cheeks were not as red as usual, nor even pink; but the trail lay again brown and silent and lonesome, with no quick hoofbeats to send the dust swirling up in a cloud.

The shadows flowed up from the gully until it was full to the brim, and threatening the golden hilltops with a brown veil of shade, before Miss Satterlee locked her door and went home. When she reached the Meekers' house she said she did not want any supper, and she said her head ached.

The third day, the schoolma'am fussed a long time with her hair, which she did in four different styles, the last being the one which Weary had praised. At noon she encouraged the children to gather wild flowers from the gully, and filled several tin cans with water from the spring and arranged bouquets with much care.

Weary loved flowers. Nearly every time he came he had a little bunch stuck under his hatband. A few of the flowers she put in her hair. She urged the children through their work and dismissed them at ten minutes of four, and told them to go straight home.

After that she swept the floor and dusted everything that could be dusted and took a few of the brightest flowers and pinned them to her white shirtwaist. The schoolma'am tuned her guitar in minor and went out and sat on the shady doorstep and waited, playing the "Battle of Waterloo" as she watched the trail and after that the "Spanish Fandango."

Tomorrow was Labor Day, and it was perfectly plain that she did not expect Weary to take her at her word. If ever a girl betrayed by every look and action that she expected to end a lovers' quarrel that evening, the schoolma'am was that girl.

At half past five—she had looked at her watch seventeen times during the last twenty minutes—a tiny cloud of dust rose over the brow of the hill. The schoolma'am stopped playing and leaned forward, breathing quickly, her gaze fixed upon that dust. The cloud grew and grew, and behind it a dark something rolled over the hilltop and followed the dust—a horseman galloping swiftly toward her.

A flush flamed in the schoolma'am's cheeks and crept from her brow down to her throat. Her fingers plucked harrowing discords from the guitar, but she didn't seem to know it; or if she did, she didn't care.

Now the horseman was near the place where he would turn off the main road and gallop straight to the schoolhouse. Glory always made that turn of his own accord. Weary had told her, only last Sunday, how he never could get Glory past that turn any more without a fight, no matter what might be the day or hour. Now he was at the turn, and without slackening that brisk lope he kept right on down the road.

The schoolma'am's hands dropped to her lap just as the blood dropped away from her cheeks and the glow dulled from her eyes. It was not Weary. It was the Swede who worked for Jim Adams and who rode a sorrel horse which, at a distance, resembled Glory very much.

Mechanically she watched him go on down the trail and out of sight. Then she picked up her guitar and went inside and closed the door and locked it. She looked around the clean, silent schoolroom, walked with echoing steps to her desk on its little platform, and laid her head down among the sweet prairie flowers and cried in the tired, heart-breaking fashion that makes a person's throat ache afterwards.

The shadows had flowed over the gully rim and the hilltops were smothered in gloom when the schoolma'am went home that night. Ma Meeker sent her straight to bed and dosed her with horrid home remedies.

By morning she had recovered her spirits—her revengeful spirit. She looked as if she were just waiting the chance to teach Weary a good lesson; but Weary did not come.

CHAPTER TWENTY-FIVE

WEARY STOOD just inside the doorway of the Dry Lake schoolhouse watching the dancers and waiting to catch Slim when he came in. For Slim, in one of his rare periods of backsliding, was, in the words of the Happy Family, pie-eyed. As a matter of family pride and loyalty they were unobtrusively riding herd on him, taking turns at the door to make sure he didn't get inside amongst the crowd and disgrace the outfit and himself.

Diplomacy had to be used plentifully, for Slim was very touchy at such times. Should he discover that he was under guard, so to speak, he would certainly raise objections that would destroy the peace and dignity of the dance.

For some obscure reason he and Joe Meeker had thrown in together earlier in the evening with two quarts of Metropole whisky—possibly more. Where they had hidden themselves away was a mystery to the boys; but that they would eventually show up at the dance was a foregone conclusion.

Weary himself had a personal reason for being concerned over the intimacy. For Slim in his cups was altogether too talkative, and if he ever got started on a certain subject, there was no telling how far he would go; and Joe Meeker was the last man in the country whom Weary would have chosen for Slim's confidant.

He stood there debating within himself whether he should go out and try once more to locate the two and separate them, or stay and risk a snub by asking the schoolma'am for the first waltz, when Cal Emmett came up and gave him a poke in the ribs by way of securing his attention.

"Say, you see that bunch of red loco over there by the organ?" he asked in a stage whisper. "That's Bert Rogers' cousin just come out from Ioway."

Weary looked in that direction and sagged back against the wall, forgetting both the schoolma'am and Slim in his surprise and consternation.

"Oh, mamma! Myrt Forsythe!" he gasped, though the name was jarred out of him in a mutter which Cal failed to catch.

"Peacherino, ain't she? Hully gee! if Len didn't have a strangle-hold on my affections I'd be making seven kinds of a fool of myself, chances is, before morning. Bert says she's a man-killer from away back."

"And that's putting it mild," Weary replied in a stunned tone. "Don't I know it!"

"Hunh? You know her?"

"I used to," Weary said dryly, and moved off, obeying the fixed, expectant stare of a pair of heavy-lidded green eyes across the room. He did not want to go; he did not really intend to go, but the first thing he knew he was standing before the girl, and she was smiling up at him just as she used to do, and there was the schoolma'am sitting near by and fanning herself vigorously with a pink feather fan, and watching him with quick little side glances.

An evil spell seemed to fall upon Weary. He heard himself telling the green-eyed girl, in a tone calculated to reach the schoolma'am's ears, that he sure was glad to

193

see her—which was a lie by the book. There was no one on earth he would have been less glad to see. He caught himself wishing that the train which had brought her to Montana had jumped the track and gone over a high bank somewhere back along the road, but what he said was, could he have the next dance?

"How strange to see *you* away out here," Miss Forsythe murmured, standing up and looking into his eyes with a little smile which implied secret understandings.

"I never knew you were Bert Rogers' cousin," Weary said as he led her out on the floor.

"I always *loved* to dance with you, Will," she murmured. "You still are the *smoothest* waltzer in the *world*."

Over the top of her head Weary's eyes were following a certain dark-haired girl who was dancing with Bert Rogers. "How long are you going to stay, Myrt?" he asked shortly.

"Well, that *depends*," she said archly. "Until after *Christmas,* anyway, I think; all *winter* if I find it sufficiently *interesting*."

"You used to have quite a knack of making things interesting for other folks," Weary murmured, staring down at the crown of Titian curls which had so ensnared him when he was seventeen.

"Did I, Will?" Myrt Forsythe laughed the little gurgling laugh in her throat which Weary had been a long while forgetting; a teasing, babyish laugh it was, and he used to think it sounded like a brook chuckling its way among stones.

It was strange that while that laugh sounded just as it always had, the effect was altogether different now, and most unpleasant. Man-killer, he thought fiercely, was right. Well she wouldn't kill him again, or anything he cared for. . . .

But before morning he was beginning to wonder a little about that. Weary never did know how she managed it, but as it turned out he found himself dancing a great many times with Myrt. Somehow he never did get a chance to dance with the schoolma'am, who was either across the room from him when the dance was called, or just going out on the floor with some other fellow. As far as he could see she was enjoying herself to the limit and had no eyes for him at all. That worried him, though you never would have guessed it from his manner.

He would have worried still more that night had he been able to hear Slim and Joe Meeker, down in a corner of the blacksmith shop where they had made themselves comfortable with their bottles and their need for seclusion, gossiping like a couple of old women.

Joe was asking Slim what the heck was the trouble between Weary and the schoolma'am, and why in thunder Weary had called off taking her to the dance? Joe said he didn't mind doing a fellow a favor, but he'd be darned if he was going to spoil his own plans again, for them or anybody else. There was a new girl working for the Wheelers, over on Dry Creek, and he had counted on bringing her to the dance. She was a Swede and her name was Emma, and while she wasn't much of a looker, she was sure friendly.

"And that's a darned sight more than you can say for

Ruby Satterlee," he added spitefully. "One of these high-toned touch-me-nots. You'd think a man's arm was a rattlesnake, by thunder, the way she shies off. And all that grammar talk—"

"Yes, and by golly, what's she got to be so stuck-up over? You'd think, by golly, a girl with a brother like that . . ." Slim had the sense to stop there, thinking of Weary.

But he had already said too much. Joe lowered the bottle he had been tilting to the smoky shop roof and leaned forward, tapping Slim impressively upon the knee.

"Yeah, she sure has got a lot to be proud of—I don't think," he sneered. "Damn train robber—that's what I heard. And her going around with her nose in the air, turning down a nice fellow like Weary."

That touched Slim. The schoolma'am oughta go down on her knees to Weary and the rest of the bunch for saving her from disgrace, he declared. He said if it hadn't been for Weary and some of the rest of the boys, she wouldn't be at the dance at all. She wouldn't want to show her face anywhere. He thought it was more than likely she would have been fired from the school and have to leave the country. Yes, by golly, and go under another name.

After that he became more general in his remarks. Between drinks he voiced many adverse opinions of human nature in general and the nature of women in particular. It was all rather jumbled, and even if Joe Meeker had been sober he might have had some difficulty in sorting out specific facts. As it was, the only thing he

196

clearly understood was that Weary had taken consider-able pains to save Johnny Satterlee from falling into the hands of the sheriff, and that he had done it for Ruby's sake, and might still get in trouble with the law if what he had done ever leaked out.

They were finishing the second bottle by then, and they drifted off into maudlin speeches about the thank-less efforts a good man would make for the sake of a woman who had a heart of stone and didn't know what gratitude meant.

Soon after that, Joe rubbed a hollow with his shoulders in a heap of sacks he had been sitting on, and leaned back muttering that the schoolma'am would come down off her perch one of these days, and would be darned glad for a friend like Joe would have been if she hadn't turned up her nose at him so much.

Slim's nice little visit with Joe was finished, and so was the second bottle. He wobbled out into the street with the hazy notion of going on up to the dance, but something gnawed at him distressingly. He thought maybe he had talked a little too freely, and if Weary found it out he would be awful mad. He thought maybe it would be just as well if he were not seen with Joe Meeker that night. It would be a good idea to get on his horse and go home and let on like he hadn't felt so good, and had left town early in the evening.

That way, he would be in the clear. No one would ever know he had seen Joe Meeker to talk to. There were sev-eral holes in that theory, but Slim was in no condition to see them. He rode out of town thinking very well of him-self, and piously resolved to steer clear of Joe in the future, stay sober and keep his big mouth shut. He really was very fond of Weary, and wouldn't have hurt him for the world.

CHAPTER TWENTY-SIX

WEARY RODE up to the schoolhouse door to find it erupting children of assorted sizes, rattling their dinner-pails as they went. Close behind the last sunbonnet came the schoolma'am, key in hand. Evidently she had no intention of lingering that evening.

Weary rode closer, smiled cheerfully down upon her and made a quick appraisement of her mood, which was going to be important, in view of what he had come to say.

"It's awful hot, Schoolma'am, for this time of year. If you'd wait a little while till the sun gets behind those clouds over there, it will be cooler to walk home."

To his secret surprise, the schoolma'am calmly sat herself down on the doorstep. Whereupon he promptly slid out of the saddle and sat down beside her, thankful that the step was not a wide one.

"You've been unmercifully hard to locate since the dance," he complained. "I just about lost my job, chasing over this way when I was supposed to be helping hold a beef herd. What was yesterday, a holiday? I came by here last night at five minutes after four, and you weren't in sight anywhere."

"You probably didn't look in the window," said the schoolma'am. "I was writing letters here until after five."

"With the door shut and locked?"

"The wind blew so," the schoolma'am explained primly. "And that lock—"

"First I knew of the wind blowing. It was hot as blue blazes when I came by. There weren't any windows up, even. Sure you were comfortable?"

"Perfectly."

Weary let that pass. "Well, where were you cached last Sunday?"

"Why, nowhere. I went with Bert Rogers and his cousin Myrtle up in the mountains. We took our lunch and had a perfectly lovely time."

"You sure got an early start, Schoolma'am. I was over at Meekers' a little after nine o'clock, thinking I could catch you at breakfast. You weren't there. So I rode the rimrock till sundown, trying to locate you. Ma Meeker said you'd gone off on a picnic, but it sure was a hard one to find. I'd rather hunt strays in the Bad Lands in a fog."

The schoolma'am seemed about to speak, but changed her mind and gazed at the purple bulk of the Bear Paws shouldering up against the sky a few miles away.

"I can't get away very easy these days," Weary went on pensively. "I wanted to come before the dance, but we were gathering some stock out the other way and I couldn't get off. We're working out from the ranch, right now, but a little later the wagons will pull out for Lonesome Prairie, and Lord knows how long we'll be gone. Beef's high this fall, and the Old Man wants to take advantage of it. He thinks the price'll drop later on; so we're gathering everything that's fit to ship."

199

The schoolma'am yawned into her palm.

"How did you like the dance?" he began again, coming straight to the subject which had brought him here.

"Lovely," said the schoolma'am, very politely.

"Glad somebody thought so," Weary said. "I drifted, right before supper."

"*Did* you?" The schoolma'am accented the first word in the way that she had taught her pupils indicated surprise.

"I didn't think you'd notice it. You were pretty busy all evening."

The schoolma'am laughed a languid assent to that.

"I never knew before that Bert Rogers was any relation to Myrt Forsythe," Weary observed, edging still closer to the vital point. "They sure aren't much alike."

"She's an old friend of yours, I believe," the schoolma'am observed.

"Well, I used to go to school with Myrt. How do you like her?"

"Lovely."

With one big spur rowel Weary began digging a little trench in the hard-packed earth. "That's what they all say about Myrt—when they first meet up with her," he observed thoughtfully.

"Including yourself, I suppose?"

"I didn't say it, I acted it," Weary grimly admitted. "From the time I was sixteen till I was most seventeen, I had about the worst case of calf love you ever saw in your life."

"How interesting!" said the schoolma'am with an

200

unconvincing little laugh.

"Yeah, it sure was. I packed a lock of her red hair in my shirt pocket and heaved sighs over it that nearly lifted me out of my boots. Then a slick-haired piano tuner came to town, and she turned those long green eyes on him. Didn't have any time for little Willie any more." He laughed reminiscently. "Darned good thing for me, too, though of course I thought my life was ruined at the time."

"I think you misunderstood Myrtle, and it wasn't the piano tuner at all. She told me—"

"Don't you ever think I misunderstood her! Not when she called me a gangling yokel—among other things. No, when Myrt and I parted for the last time we sure understood each other perfectly."

"But it couldn't have been actually necessary for you to sneak away—"

The tolerant little smile left Weary's mouth. "That word sneak is one I never had fired at me before," he said in a new tone. "What has that damned redhead been telling you?"

"Mr. Davidson, I didn't think you'd swear about a woman!"

"I suppose it gives evidence of a low brutal trait in my nature that you hoped I wouldn't harbor," Weary observed, altogether too mildly.

"It certainly does," snapped the schoolma'am, her cheeks flushing.

Weary silently raked up the sunbaked soil with his spur. "Myrt's the kind of girl that makes men swear about women," he said shortly.

"It seems almost a pity sometimes that women haven't the same privilege of expressing themselves forcibly as men do," she retorted.

"Oh, Myrt can do a pretty fair job of cussing, herself, when she gets started. I found that out when we were having words about the piano tuner." He turned his head and looked straight at the schoolma'am. "What did you mean about me sneaking away," he demanded, "and what have you been up on your ear about, lately? Still mad about the gopher?"

The schoolma'am looked at him and looked away again. "The incident of the murdered gopher," she said distinctly, "was merely an indication of certain fundamental weaknesses which I can no longer ignore."

"Oh."

"I wouldn't say that I am up on my ear, as you so elegantly put it. I am merely disillusioned, Mr. Davidson. Thoroughly disillusioned. I had thought you were my friend, and I find you are not. You gave me some very good advice—at least it was plausible and seemed good at the time—and then I find that you not only gossip about my family affairs, but you fail to keep your promise to me. I am speaking," she said hardly, "about Johnny."

Weary gave an audible gasp of astonishment. "Johnny? What's Johnny got to do with it?"

"A great deal," the schoolma'am said shortly. "You were very urgent that I should not take any steps to find Johnny and persuade him to go back to school where he belongs. You said he was on his own, and that it would make a man of him. Now," she added bitterly, "I find his name bandied about the country. It seems that he is accused of disgracing himself in some way which no one seems to know; and that you either started the gossip or made it your business to peddle the rumor afterwards. And if you call *that* being a friend, your idea of friendship is very different from mine."

They were both standing now, facing each other with a calm kind of fury. "Just where did you hear so much?" Weary asked sharply. "From Joe, I suppose?"

"Does it matter? You persuaded me to let Johnny go. Why, I can't imagine, now. I believed you were thinking of my welfare and his. I thought, of course, that if you heard anything at all about him you would certainly tell me, instead of peddling it all over the country."

"Did Joe tell you I peddled—"

"Joe really told me very little," she said in her haughtiest tone. "He said if I wanted to know where Johnny was and what he was up to I could ask you."

"Oh. He did, hunh?"

"I had taken it for granted, Mr. Davidson, that it would not be necessary to ask you if you knew where Johnny was. I was fool enough to believe that you would give me any information that happened to come your way. I—trusted you."

The quiver in her voice made Weary look at her quickly and look away again. "You might," he said in a low tone, "do worse than to go right on trusting me."

"I don't see how. I was a fool to trust you in the first place." Her cold dignity broke without warning. She took a step toward him and stood with her hands clenched at her sides, and her eyes flashing such anger

203

as he had never seen in them before, or ever wanted to see again.

"Since the whole country seems to know where my brother is and what he is doing," she said harshly, "I think I am entitled to know, also. I will not endure this conspiracy of hints and evasions any longer. *Where is Johnny?* I want his address. What is all this gossip that's going around about him? Is he in trouble?" That last question was wrung from her pride and her fear.

Weary half turned, looped Glory's reins up over the horse's head and lifted a foot to the stirrup.

"Aren't you going to tell me?"

From the saddle he looked down upon her with unsmiling eyes. "No." His tone was level and there was that quality in it which boded ill for somebody. "So long as you take that stand, there's no use telling you a thing. You don't trust me an inch, I can see that. Looks to me like you never did trust me."

"Will Davidson, I hate you! You've ruined my brother's chance to be somebody! I could have found him—I could have brought him back to school. I would have, only for you. I wish I never had seen you! If anything happens to Johnny, it will be your fault!"

"If that's the way you feel, Schoolma'am, I've got nothing to say. Just go right ahead and take Joe's word for it. Don't wait to find out if it's true, just swallow it anyway."

"Of course it's true. If it weren't, you'd say so!"

"Would I?" Weary gave her a long, intent look. "Well, good-by—be good to yourself." He leaned to one side, swung back his feet without actually touching Glory with the spurs; and the horse wheeled and with one jump was out of sight around the corner of the schoolhouse.

The schoolma'am stood there watching until horse and rider flashed into view on the road. She watched them out of sight over the brow of the hill. Then she sat down on the doorstep and buried her face in her hands.

CHAPTER TWENTY-SEVEN

SLIM, OF course—Slim and Joe Meeker and two bottles of whisky. . . . He ought to have known what would happen when those two got off together. It was his own fault—what he should have done was collar Slim right at the start when he first saw them with their heads together in Rusty's place.

Whisky talk. . . . He didn't know as he could blame Slim so much; Slim had kept his mouth shut all summer; they all had. Whatever he had told Joe, it wasn't the truth. Or if it was, Joe had had sense enough not to pass it on to the schoolma'am; but he had passed something—enough, and more than enough.

Slim and Myrt Forsythe. . . . Between the two of them they had certainly managed to stir up a fine mess. For the first ten miles of hard riding and hard thinking, Weary was in the mood to take Slim apart, just about. Before he had reached camp, however, his temper changed, cooled. What was done was done. Jumping Slim's carcass now wouldn't help any. All it could do would be to make things worse, spread the story like a prairie fire.

Stir up more talk, and the truth was bound to come out. Better let the schoolma'am go on thinking he had double-crossed her. She'd get over that. He couldn't fool himself into believing it would break her heart or anything like that. And it left her thinking maybe Johnny wasn't so bad.

Weary didn't want any supper that night. He didn't want to talk, either. He saddled a fresh horse and went off to stand guard over the herd, and during his allotted time he rode round and round the quiet cattle, staring straight out over his horse's head and seeing nothing but his own bitter hurt. Not that he neglected his work—he did that mechanically. Turning back a restless steer trying to leave the bunch, he did not remember the next minute what he had done.

At first he thought he would pull out and say nothing to anyone. It was what he wanted to do, all right enough. Some men would have done it, but not Weary. He stayed with the roundup, did his job and went his way—more silent than the Happy Family had ever known him to be. No elaborate jokes played on anyone. None of that give-and-take heckling when the boys were lying around camp before they turned in at night.

Pink noticed the difference, and so did Chip and Jack Bates. The others did not pay so much attention, being more or less self-centered individuals, chiefly concerned with their own little interests; but they were working short-handed and the shipping was heavy; there wasn't much time to wonder over a man's moods.

It seemed to Weary that he kept his feelings strictly to himself. He was careful not to show any coolness towards Slim, even. He worked until the shipping was over. Then he went to the Old Man and asked for his time, giving no definite reason other than to say he wanted a change.

The Happy Family were considerably indignant and wasted much profanity and useless argument in trying to change his mind, but it seemed to Weary that he warded off their curiosity and their questions very adroitly. He declared over and over that he was sick of punching cows, and he wasn't hankering to shovel hay another winter to a bunch of ungrateful bawling calves. When Pink protested, Weary reminded him how he had felt the very self-same way not so long ago.

He wanted a change of scenery; he just wanted to knock around and get the alkali dust out of his lungs and see something grow besides calves and cactus. When they badgered him further, he looked them in the eye and explained that one thing he had always meant to settle to his own satisfaction was whether apples actually grew with little squares of paper wrapped around them. Oranges, too; he said he always did have his doubts about oranges growing yellow and barenaked on a tree, and he might sashay out to California and prowl through an orange grove and find out for himself.

When was he coming back? Well, now, that was a question. Mamma! He hadn't even got started yet. He wasn't figuring on the coming-back part; what he was interested in was the getting started.

He didn't waste much time over that. The night after the last car door was pushed shut past the rump of the last Flying U steer to be loaded, the Happy Family rode in a body to the station to see Weary off. They looked rather forlorn, standing there on the platform on a bright moonlight night, the planks squeaking with frost under their boot-heels. But they didn't act forlorn; they yelled advice, good and bad, and when the train was ready to start they piled on their horses and galloped alongside it and emptied their six-shooters into the air, yipping and yelling until the Pullman windows were filled with shocked faces.

Weary stood on the rear platform and waved his hat as long as a rider was in sight. After that he went into the smoker, found a place where he could stretch his long legs over two seats, made himself a cigarette and forgot to smoke it while he watched the gray plains slide behind him under the moon. After a while a fellow who traveled for a San Francisco wine house spoke to him pleasantly, and Weary thrust his thoughts from him and set his face to the future.

He had talked California, but he didn't go there after all. He went to Portland, Oregon, instead. He had money in his pocket, and for a while he just moseyed around getting acquainted with the town. He wasn't so conspicuous as he had feared he would be, for cowboys frequently came in off the Eastern Oregon ranges to spend their money hilariously and go back again to earn more.

For a while he liked the feeling of being just one of the herd, never hearing his name called on the street or looking into a pair of eyes that answered back. No one knew who he was, and no one cared. People hurried past him without a glance in his direction. He didn't have to answer personal questions, or satisfy anyone's curiosity about why he never wanted to see the schoolma'am any more. It sure was a relief.

After a while he took a run up to Seattle, having some vague notion of giving the Klondike a whirl. He wandered up and down the waterfront, and watched the big boats load for distant ports. It was interesting, all right, but somehow he never did book passage on one of them. It was the wrong time of year, for one reason. The boats were getting out of the Klondike for the winter, they weren't going in. If any of them had, it is very likely Weary would have been on one of them. He played with the idea. Later he almost accepted a job driving a meat truck for a big packing company. He could work at that until spring, he thought, and then go north.

But he didn't. Instead, he returned to Portland. The big boats came in there, too, but the town lacked the full flavor of Seattle—and he liked it better. For a while it pleased him to walk the streets grown familiar in his first weeks of exile. There was something friendly about going into the same restaurant to eat, or idling before a harness shop he knew.

But that didn't last long. He was not an idler by nature, and presently he found himself looking for work. There wasn't much he could do in a city. He tried digging ditches, along with a motley crew of mixed nationalities—culled from all breeds he decided. The first day he blistered both hands and got a crick in his back, and the second day he quit.

On the third day he brought up at the door of a livery stable. A man stood spraddled in the doorway, one hand deep in his pocket and the other punctuating the remarks he was making to a droop-shouldered hostler. Some of the remarks were interesting in the extreme and Weary frankly listened, glad they were not directed at himself. The droop-shouldered man presently slunk away, and Weary took his place before the proprietor.

"Looks like you've got a vacancy on your hands," he said in his pleasant drawl. "If you have, I'd like to try it a whirl."

The man measured Weary up and down with his eyes, and there being a good deal of Weary measured length-wise, several seconds were consumed in the inspection.

"Hunh! What do you know about horses?" The question was not as unreasonable as it would seem. In Seattle, Weary had found himself rather conspicuous in range garb, and so had staked himself to an outfit of town clothes and another suitcase for his big hat and boots and what went with them. At a glance he bore none of the earmarks of the range as he stood looking down on the other man.

"If you aren't going to be busy for a while, I'll start right in and tell you what I know about horses," he replied amiably. "Better sit down on that bucket while I'm doing it, though, because if I'm thorough it'll take some time."

The man sliced off the end of a black cigar with one vicious bite. "You seem to think you know it all. What's your trade?"

"Punching cows—in northern Montana."

The man took the trouble to look at him again. "Bron-cobuster?"

"Some," Weary grinned, his thoughts whirling back to the dust and uproar in the Flying U corral, and to his many little arguments with Glory.

"You ought to know better than to founder a three-hun-dred-dollar trotter, then," the man remarked, some of the harshness gone from his voice.

"I sure had," Weary agreed.

"I need men here that know a little something about horses. Pay is good—I won't have a man in the stable that can't earn good wages. Go tell the foreman I've hired you—back there in the office. Give you a try-out, anyway."

So Weary found a job and stayed with it. It gave him a foothold, something to think about besides the necessity of pushing his thoughts from him.

He never wrote back to the Flying U, except once when he had first landed in Seattle. A short letter, that was, addressed to Percival Cadwolloper Perkins at the Flying U, but meant for the entire outfit.

He was looking over the corral of boats, he told them. Figured on climbing aboard a nice gentle one and riding the billows for a change. From all accounts, a fellow could look for some rough riding out on the bounding main, and when he got to the Klondike, should he send them back an iceberg, or would they rather have a nugget big as your fist for a stickpin? He'd try and gather a flock of nuggets by Christmas time.

It was intended to be a very funny letter, but no one laughed very much when they read it. About all they got from it was the chilling fact that Weary was headed for the Klondike—the jumping-off place, as far as the Happy Family was concerned. Weary hadn't remem-bered to give any specific address, so the round-robin letter mailed immediately back to General Delivery,

Seattle, went uncalled for and finally wound up in the Dead Letter Office and stayed there; for the Happy Family had not thought of putting on a return address, either. Good Lord! Weary knew where to write, didn't he?

Weary knew, well enough, but somehow he never availed himself of the knowledge. After all that guff about the Klondike and the gold nuggets big as your fist, he didn't like to say he was working in a livery stable in Portland. They'd give him the laugh if they found that out. Furthermore, he didn't want the news to reach the schoolma'am's ears.

It was a good job, as jobs went—but just on the face of it he knew it would sound like quite a comedown, after the Klondike. In the Klondike, anything could happen. A man could spend the winter up there and come back rich. . . . And he had to admit that playing nursemaid to a bunch of broke horses in a stable carried nothing to stimulate the imagination.

Let it ride. It gave him the blues, anyway, just to think of writing back. Forget it. A man had to play his own hand out, and he had best play it alone.

CHAPTER TWENTY-EIGHT

MYRT FORSYTHE stayed until after Christmas, as was her plan. The schoolma'am had another tree and a short program, in which only the school children took part, and in the opinion of the Happy Family the whole thing was flat as a cold pancake. They guessed the rest of the crowd liked it all right, but they knew darned well the schoolma'am didn't get much kick out of it herself. Beyond herding the kids one by one to the platform where they recited their pieces, she kept herself pretty much in the background.

No doubt about it, the schoolma'am had lost weight in the last few weeks. Even Slim noticed that. She was keeping pretty much to herself and not going to any dances or surprise parties, and her eyes were too big for her face.

Pink stood it as long as he could. That was a week or so after New Year's when Joe Meeker had tried to pump him about Johnny Satterlee. As it turned out, Joe gave more information than he got, and Pink thought he saw what lay behind Weary's sudden departure. Pink was the kind who believed in action, but, on the other hand, he had sense enough to see that this was a mighty ticklish matter which required careful handling.

The first thing he did was to get Slim off in a corner by himself and find out exactly how much he had told Joe. After that he spent another day or two in deep thought, and a full evening writing a letter in the mess house where he wouldn't be disturbed.

The next day, a little after four o'clock in the afternoon, he rode up to the schoolhouse, dismounted like a young man with an errand to perform, and walked in without knocking. His eyes were as blue as the sky outside, and nearly as cold. His cheeks were pink as a girl's, and he showed no sign of dimples.

The schoolma'am, halfway through her sweeping, stopped dead-still and leaned on the broom, both hands clasped over the end of the handle. Her face turned red

213

and then white, and she didn't say a word.

Pink drew off his fleece-lined gloves and spread his fingers to the heat still radiating up from the stove. "I don't suppose you've heard from Weary, lately," he said in his soft voice which somehow had an edge to it.

"No, I haven't. Have you?" The schoolma'am couldn't keep a certain amount of eagerness from her tone, but she added, "I didn't expect to hear. Why should I?"

"You shouldn't. Not after the way you treated him."

"I beg your pardon?"

"You needn't. It's Weary's pardon you'd better beg, if you ever get the chance."

The schoolma'am lifted her chin at that. "I fail to see why. Mr. Davidson has certainly not shown himself my friend—on the contrary—"

"You mean about Johnny?"

The schoolma'am took a sharp breath. "Yes, I mean about Johnny. Before he left, Mr. Davidson certainly—"

Pink loosened the tabs of his sealskin cap with a jerk of the strings. "He certainly didn't deserve the raw deal you handed him, Miss Satterlee. I don't know how much you heard about him and Johnny, but whatever it was, it was a darned lie. Away back last June . . ."

Then Pink told her. He was merciless, and he omitted nothing. Before he finished the schoolma'am was crumpled up in one of the desk seats, the broom lying lengthwise in the aisle, and her hands were pressed hard against her face and her eyes. But she was very quiet—she scarcely seemed to breathe.

"And that's why Weary never came to the picnic," Pink finished. "He made believe he found that money on the ground, tied up in Johnny's handkerchief, and he made the trip to Billings and turned it over to the bank. He let 'em think—"

"Stop it! *Stop it!* I can't bear any more!"

"Oh yes you can. You're going to hear the rest of it now." Pink reached into his pocket and drew out a letter. "I've got it all thought out, Miss Satterlee. I've got a letter here that's supposed to come from Canada. You don't have to show the envelope to anybody, but the letter oughta be proof enough to make any granny-gossip around here shut their mouth about Johnny."

"I just can't believe—"

"You'd better believe what's in this letter, then. I've got a friend over in Canada, Rowdy Vaughn. I used his name. I'm going to write to him and put him wise, so if anybody tries to check up he'll be ready for 'em."

He hesitated, looking at the schoolma'am's bowed head.

"You needn't read the letter right now," he said, more kindly. "It's supposed to be from Rowdy, telling you about how your brother that had been working for him just died of pneumonia. It says here that the kid used another name (I thought it better be that way in case any smart guy gets nosin' around up there) and didn't let on who he was or where he come from till he got sick. Then he told Rowdy about you, and that's why Rowdy wrote."

"But why—?"

"Josephine!" Pink exclaimed with an exasperated kind of pity. "You oughta see why, all right. This way, you can go ahead and mourn for Johnny all you want to. You can show this letter to anybody that acts like they doubt your word. It says Johnny was up there all last spring—that lets him out on any train or bank robbery. All the talk that's been going around about Johnny is just guesswork anyway. This oughta put the kibosh on it for good and all."

The schoolma'am took down her hands and looked at him with her tragic brown eyes. "I'll never forgive myself—"

"I guess you acted according to your lights," Pink conceded. "If Weary ever comes back, try and treat him white. That's all I ask." He laid the letter on the desk before her, pulled on his gloves, tied his cap and left her there without another word.

CHAPTER TWENTY-NINE

PORTLAND WAS having a spell of weather. Through the first part of the winter there had been snow and sleet, and after that sunshine, then slashing storms of wind and rain when the water ran in the streets and streetcars were stalled in the lower part of town. Weary didn't mind that so much. It was very much what he had expected of the climate, and he insisted to himself that he was darned glad to get away from the blizzards of Montana.

But later in the season came this fog and rain which never reached the proportions of a downpour and yet never quite ceased the distressing drip and drizzle. A few days of it wouldn't have mattered so much, but it went on and on, till it seemed as if the sun never would shine again. The streets were drab and dull, a place of bobbing umbrellas, muddy crossings, sloppy pavement and dripping eaves, with a cold that chilled the marrow of his bones.

He had enough to do to keep him busy from five o'clock in the morning, when he worked under dim bulbs of electric light, to six o'clock in the evening when he went off shift. Hours of feeding hungry horses their breakfasts; brushing, currying, combing till their hair shone satin-smooth; harnessing, unharnessing; washing the mud from rigs that would be splashed and plastered again before night. . . . Driving to houses that were known by the number over the door, leaving the team for somebody to use, and walking back in the rain; piling mangers with hay, strewing the stalls deep with straw; patting this horse as he passed, commanding the next one to move over, stopping to whisper caressing words into the ear of a favorite. . . . In the evening, sitting listlessly in the balcony of some theater—or more often in his dingy bedroom on the third floor of a cheap boardinghouse on Second Street.

To a fellow fresh from eating, sleeping, working, reveling with those who would cheerfully give him the coats from their backs if he needed them; fight for him, laugh at him or with him, tease him, bully him, love him like a brother—in short, fresh from the Flying U outfit and the Happy Family—that winter in Portland was not exactly hilarious.

No one hailed him as Weary. His fellow hostlers just simply called him Bill. No one knew the life he knew, or loved the things he loved. The stories of his adventures never were told, because he would have had to explain them as he went along, and he couldn't quite see himself doing that.

Sometimes he would sit all evening in his damp-walled room and smoke cigarettes and wonder what the boys were doing down in the bunkhouse. He wondered if they were keeping Glory up in the pasture, or if he was rustling on the range, back humped to the storm and the deviltry gone out of him with the grim battle for life.

Maybe there was a dance somewhere. Happy Jack would wear the same red necktie and the same painful smile of embarrassment, and there would be a squabble over the piece of bar mirror to shave by, and the school-ma'am—but at that point Weary's thoughts would shy away from Montana. Even after so long a time he could not bring himself to think of the schoolma'am.

January, February, March—spring had come in Portland and the fruit trees were in bloom. Weary began to whistle once more as he went about his work. He never whistled "Good Old Summertime," but there were other foolish songs becoming popular. He rather fancied "Navajo" these days. He liked his work, and the pay was good. He learned the ways of the town, began to make friends; not close friends—no Cadwolloper or Chip or Cal, or any of the rest of the boys, but fellows who were all right in their way, and who came to fill his days with a sense of belonging. As he had once told himself with a bitter kind of humor, he had quit bawling and gone to eating hay.

April came, and Portland was at her best. Weary had been to a dance last night with some of the boys, and had enjoyed himself hugely. There were lots of pretty girls in

Portland, and a fellow could have a good time if he wanted it, and didn't hang off by himself all the time.

"Nava, Nava, my Navajo!
I have a love for you that will gro-ow,"

Weary sang melodiously while he spread the straw bedding in the stalls with his fork. He was thinking of a girl he had danced with a good deal last night; a little blonde who was sure light on her feet as a feather, and had a very cute way of saying the last thing you'd expect her to say. Weary thought he might speak for a horse and buggy for next Sunday afternoon, and take her for a drive around in the parks:

"If you'll have a coon for a beau,
I'll be your Navajo!"

he finished the ditty as he snapped the wires off a bale of hay and tore it open in a hurry to finish.

A familiar, pungent odor smote his nostrils, and he straightened. For a minute he stood perfectly still; then his fingers groped in the hay, closed upon something, and every nerve in him quivered.

It was a branch of sagebrush, dry, pressed flat, some of the finer twigs broken—but it nevertheless carried its message bravely. He held it in his hand and sat down limply upon the torn bale of hay, holding that bit of sage cupped between his palms, close to his face.

As he closed his eyes and inhaled the tangy odor he knew and loved, gray plains seemed to spread out before him; the dear, familiar rangeland, carved and broken with sharp-nosed hills and deep, water-worn gullies lying barren and yellow in the sun. The blue sky was bending down to meet the hills, with feathery white clouds trailing lazily across. The cool winds slapped his hatbrim and tingled his blood. His knees felt the splendid working muscles of a galloping horse.

Now he was racing over the springy sod, the sweet smell of bruised grass in his nostrils. Wild range cattle lumbered out of his way, ran a few paces and stopped to gaze after him with curious eyes. Before him stood the white-tented camp of the roundup, and the corral was filled with circling horses half-hidden by the veil of dust thrown up by their restless, battling hoofs.

Now he was in the midst of them, a coil of rope in his left hand; his right swinging the loop over his head. Choking dust was in his eyes and throat and he loved it. Men were shouting to one another above the confusion of milling horses. Oaths were hurled after some horses which had dodged their loops. Saddles strewed the ground, spurs jingled, carefree laughter brightened the general clamor.

Now he was sitting on the schoolhouse steps holding a smoking gun in his hand, and the schoolma'am was standing flushed and indignant before him. . . . She was accusing him of something far from the truth; telling him he was no friend of hers—he had double-crossed her about Johnny. . . .

"What's the matter, Bill? Yuh sick?"

Weary raised his haggard face from his hands. The plains, the blue sky, the sunshine, the wind, the girl—

gone. He was sitting upon a torn bale of hay in a livery stable in Portland. In his fingers was a crumpled bit of gray sagebrush.

"You look sick," the foreman repeated sympathetically. "Wanta knock off the rest of the day?"

Weary got unsteadily to his feet and walked away. He was all right, he said, gruffly for him; he lifted the bale of hay upon his strong back and carried it away to a manger. In his pocket the broken branch of sage sent its nostalgic message to his nostrils. It was the message of the open ranges; a message straight from the Flying U; straight from the schoolma'am, waiting on the schoolhouse steps.

Late that night, Weary started home. In his coat pocket, where his fingers touched it often, lay the crumpled piece of sagebrush. Dry it was, and the gray leaves were crumbling under the homesick touch of his fingers. . . . But the smell of it, aromatic and strong, helped to make the journey bearable.

Since his train was the first out of Portland headed for the direction he wanted to travel, he had taken the Northern route. At Kalispell he went out and stood on the platform and filled his lungs again and again with good old Montana air. The sun shone, the skies were blue, and the clouds reminded him of a band of new-washed sheep scattered over their feeding ground.

At Shelby, half a dozen cowboys galloped briefly into view and headed down the valley, and Weary raised his car window and leaned far out to look after them with hungry eyes. He wanted to swing his hat and give a whoop at sight of them, but he didn't. He caught the unfriendly eye of other passengers who didn't like drafts and closed the window.

He wished now that he had written to some of the boys and kept himself posted on what was happening back home. It seemed years that he had been away. No matter—he was on his way back. He'd darned soon find out what was what.

The schoolma'am had just finished hearing the last spelling class recite when she glanced out through the window and saw Glory, bearing a familiar figure, race down to the turn and whip into the schoolhouse path.

She caught at the desk to steady herself and hung on so hard the knuckles of that hand were white as milk. But she had presence of mind, nevertheless. "School's dismissed!" she said sharply. "Attention—turn—stand—pass."

The children eyed her curiously, hesitated and then rushed noisily outside, and the schoolma'am sat down abruptly with her face in her hands. Outside she could hear them shouting, "Hello, Weary!" in a dozen different voices. Each time she heard that name her heart gave a jump.

Then spurred heels clanked on the threshold, stopped there while the door was shut with a bang. The schoolma'am did not look up; perhaps she did not dare. Steps came down the room toward her; long, hurrying steps; determined steps. Beside the desk they stopped, and for a space that seemed endless there was no sound.

"Won't you say hello to me, Schoolma'am?"

"Hello," the schoolma'am said faintly, her hands still hiding her face.

Weary stood for another minute, then he reached out and pulled down her hands. "Look up here, Schoolma'am," he commanded. "I've come back to fight it out to a finish. You can't stampede me again, so you needn't try."

"I don't—want to," the schoolma'am confessed meekly, giving him one brief glance.

The next she knew she was standing up with Weary's arms around her. Her face was being tilted backwards and Weary's lips were hard against her mouth.

"Say you're *my* little schoolma'am. Quick, before I do it again!"

"I'm your—oh—Will! I nearly *died* wanting you to come back!"

"I did die, Schoolma'am. Died and buried myself." Weary was talking against her hair. "Then I came back for the Judgment Day. Mamma!" he breathed, lifting his head and looking around the schoolroom and out through the window at the dreaming hills. "You don't know how good it is to be back."

"I guess I do know," quavered the schoolma'am. Suddenly her arms were up around his neck and she was clinging as if for her very life. "Oh, I deserved to lose you, but I can't! I mustn't! Promise me, Will—don't *ever* go again and leave me!"

Weary's answer, while perfectly satisfactory, was not made with words.

Center Point Publishing
600 Brooks Road • PO Box 1
Thorndike ME 04986-0001 USA

(207) 568-3717

US & Canada:
1 800 929-9108